Legends, Folktales, and Other Stories

A novella
Written by S. G. Lee
First Edition 2017

SB

An imprint of Shillelagh Books
London, Ontario, Canada

Acknowledgments:
Sincere thanks to Jodi and Sydney, without your constant support and encouragement, this book would not be possible. You are the best friends a writer could have. I dedicate this book to my daughters, my son-in law and my husband; who have supported my writing endeavours with encouragement and love. Special thanks to my beloved mother in heaven, who taught me dreams, can come true with hard work, perseverance and patience.

Published at CreateSpace
Copyright © 2017 by Sheilagh G. Lee
All Rights Reserved
ISBN (13) 978-1-987977-16-5 (paperback)
ISBN-10:1987977165
ISBN 978-1-987977-15-8 (e-book)

Table of Contents

Preface: A Note from the Folk Teller

I've always enjoyed the romance and the pageantry of folktales, myths and legends. There is something about stepping into other worlds of fairies and kings and princesses that makes it interesting and fun to read.

I hope you will find my stories a place to escape to as I did with those I read when I was young or that my grandmother told me at her knee. What are you waiting for? Turn the page and begin...

Call to the Water

I call her to the water
This child so beautiful
Her hair long and dark hangs down
Her limbs long and wiry
Beckoning her
To the water's edge
I play for her my ancient shell
Hearing the siren song
Of my aquatic home
I reach for her
My pelt disappears
A boy in love
With a young girl
She's drawn back
Year after year
Searching for me
I smile, take her hand
For one day a year
She's mine
Bound together
Her eighteenth year
I make her mine
Guard your girl children well
For my young son hunts a spouse
A pretty little girl
Who will grow into a woman
He can call bride
~0~

Selkie

A young handsome and strong farmer, Adhamh who lived in the town of An Innis farmed day and night and his parents despaired of him ever finding a bride. Toiling the field he stared across the distance and felt compelled to walk to the beach. Watching the object he saw a woman strode out of the waves, discarded whatever was the black behind a rock on the beach. The woman, Segna had hair black and long which hung to her waist and eyes black and piercing. The farmer instantly smitten instinctively hid the black object she discarded in a trunk. Not long after he married her.

Segna seemed happy at first, but soon told her husband though she loved him, she longed for the sea. She was a Selkie, even if it meant she must be parted from him forever, she must go, but she couldn't find the pelt she knew he hid.

Adhamh who loved the earth and farming, he feared never seeing her again. In the end as Segna grew paler and weaker he relented and gave her back her pelt. Segna who loved him told him that he could come with her, but he would never see the earth again, but live forever. Adhamh made a decision.

"Are you sure you want to do this?" Segna asked.
"Yes," Adhamh answered.

So if you see two seals bobbing in the Scottish seas, you may be seeing the one of the greatest love stories ever told Adhamh and Segna.

~0~

Tradition

T radition is a great thing they tell you, but not when

that practice will steal your life from you. Today the whole village awaited outside my house to take me to my doom.

I'm not making sense you say. Of course I'm not. I'm scared and the noise from their shouting to me to come out of my hut scares me.

Every year one maiden is chosen to give to the beast to placate him and keep our village safe from harm. To make it fair each maiden reaches in a bag made from a sheep's intestine and pulls out a stone only one is painted red. We'd chosen our stones yesterday and unfortunately I had chosen the red one from the bag.

I turned to my mother and begged, "Tell me I'm not giving my life away for nothing."
"You must obey." my mother counselled "A great honor has been bestowed on our family. You will save our village."
"Honor all this talk about honor! Don't you care that you will never see me again?"
"I care, but this is your destiny, I cannot change it," mother answered tears filling her eyes.
"No fate is not something we can escape."
"I love you now go meet your purpose," mother cried.

After a few minutes mother left to join the crowd and tell them I would join them soon. I tucked two knives into sleeves upon my thighs and strapping two to each of my forearms. When mother returned, I was bathed and anointed with scents, dressed in finery bound with ribbons and then escorted in great ceremony to the monsters cave.

My eyes struggled to adjust to darkness, in the corner a giant of a man lay snoring. He awoke abruptly threw back his head and began laughing when he saw me.

"Another virgin sacrificed to the Beast?" he asked.

"You aren't a monster," I commented trying to mollify the creature.

"Aren't I?"

"Let me go. I will travel far away. No one will know."

"Like all the others you expect me to let you go?"

"Others?"

"Did you think I devoured them as the Beast?"

"If you didn't, why are there bones in the corner?"

"Perceptive little Beauty, aren't you? I'm going back to my nap don't attempt to leave. I might be hungry later."

Waiting for him to start breathing heavily in sleep, I listened to every sound. When he began snoring I then went to him. He awoke and grabbed me binding me with rope, than placing me in a corner went back to his pallet to sleep. I managed to slide a knife down my forearm slicing the rope that held me. Pretending sleep I watched his chest rise and fall. At dusk as he turned slowly into a Beast and I stabbed him four times in the heart. There will be no more sacrifices. 'Beauty Slayed the Beast' is my legendary story.

~0~

I want to be a Valkyrie

"I wanna be a Valkyrie!" the fourteen year old princess complained.

"In four years, Eir," replied her eighteen year old Aunt Svipul.

"When do you get to be one?"

"I already am. I decide the fates of those in battle," Svipul answered.

"Then you take some to Fólkvangr?"

"Yes, they are picked for Ragnarök when they shall help repopulate the world."

"I don't understand they are men they can't repopulate anything," protested Eir.

"That is why they need us."

"Did they let you take Grímnismál?"

"My horse is with me."

"I want to take Darraðarljóð but he may not be ready in time."

"Grímnismál had a lot of training. He flies through the air dodging weapons helping me save the chosen. Tonight I can just be Princess Svipul, but the battle begins tomorrow, so I must go.

"You are a Valkyrie, how could you want to be anything else?"Eir demanded.

"Being a Valkyrie is an esteemed job, but the men drain your energy to retain theirs. They demand much of you."

"I don't understand."

"You will. You'll wish you hadn't been born a Valkyrie. Deciding who dies and who gets to go to Fólkvangr is taxing."

"You make it sound like a job; but we will be remembered forever."

"Will we? Do you remember any of the others?" asked Svipul.

"But we are heroes,"Eir protested.

"It has always been men who decide who are the winners and the losers. Men decide who are heroes, until we take that back we will never be remembered."

"When I am a Valkyrie they will remember. I will make them."

"I believe they will Eir. You are unforgettable,"Svipul declared.

Not long after Eir got her wish and became remembered forever more.

"For In the Poetic Edda poem Fjölsvinnsmál wrote Eir is remembered."

~0~

Pele

Wahieloa is gone. The woman who shares only part of my name shall not take him. My son Menehune requires his father. I desire Wahieloa to keep me calm and warm my bed. I search steadfastly my anger growing. How could he betray me like this? He had crawled into our bed with her, Pele-kumu-honua. Why was I not enough? Did I not cater to his every whim and become a shadow of myself for him. I could not be a shadow anymore I was fire and light wind and rain. I was water flowing in a torrent. How could he want the pale copy of me?

I need more time to convince Wahieloa of his mistake, but the storm rises in my head and I have no control. A sea of sharks rises from my head and thrice rises over hill and isle then recedes. To my remorse I have killed them both. But I still have my son. I, Pele shall mother him and he shall arise a great God. Menehune was a master craftman. He would surpass both his parents. He could already create fishponds and temple buildings. He would make me proud. I was content. I could rest for awhile.

~0~

Recruit

"She's dead!"

"We weren't given a choice Ariel. Our job is not an easy one."

"I wasn't recruited like you, I was tricked."

"I've read your file. You're lucky they didn't imprison you, or put you on the S.O.S. list."

"Shoot on sight, isn't that a bit extreme?"

"Ariel, a dangerous beast needs to be put down."

"Do you call me a beast?" Ariel stared hard at Jâzâ urging him to take it back. Ariel's teeth elongated, her eyes popping out and protruding.

"Pull it back wolf," Jâzâ cried his skin turning red and his muscles bulging in his chest. Two horns appeared on his head and a long forked tail appearing at his back.

"You're Semjâzâ,"Ariel cried in shock.

"I am the legendary, Semjâzâ. Mere mortals think I rule over angels but the truth is I decide their fate. Now you will too, that is when I let you."

"I thought they forced you to be my partner too."

"No, I recruited you. My people brought you to me and I decided to test the beast, instead of shooting you on sight."

"Did I pass?" Ariel asked.

"That remains to be seen but your remorse was noted. Now onto our next target the black beast of Echlor."

"Will we kill this one like we did the woman Centaur?"

"If the beast charges with a sword or any weapon we'll kill it. If it lays down we'll recruit it."

"Now, I feel like a Vampire slayer," Ariel complained.

"Good, that might save you."

And so they slayed the black beast of Echlor and Ariel became the King's knight, his wolf of choice protecting the kingdom.

~0~

Red Mist

T he pea soup fog slithered in devouring buildings
roads and people alike. Mom and dad forbid me from going
out, but it called to me. Teens shouldn't be kept in because
of a little fog; besides I had a party to go to. Sneaking out
the back door, I entered the fog thinking of all the stories of
evil my parents had told me. I took to my heels and ran
towards my destination, hitting something hard. My body
rolled end over end. Something pinned me down and tried
to harm me. I fought back tearing them limb from limb and
eating the liver and kidneys I craved. When it was all over
six men lay dead in front of me. I heard sirens and I ran
home. I tried to open the front door, but my hands wouldn't
work. Grandfather appeared at the door holding it open,
staring at me and I went in.
"So it's happened," he said, "Don't feel bad granddaughter,
it's what they deserve."
"I killed them. They didn't deserve that."
"There is one rule for all, my child, survival of the fittest."
"But what will happen now that they know what I am?"
"They are dead. They've never found me, I'm the Ripper.
The one they fear the most," grandfather answered.
With this I felt my body calm and felt myself return to
normal.
"How long has our family had this affliction?"
"It's not an affliction, but a calling we become one with the
fog and must feed. Now rest child until the next red mist
calls."

Regulus Slayer of Dragons

I couldn't believe my eyes on the opposite side of the street I saw a sight to behold. Most people seeing him saw a nerdy man with glasses in a blue checked shirt and loafers; I with the gift of my third eye, I saw him for what he really was a slayer of dragons. As I watched from the shadows lurked a dragon. I continued to watch; even with my third eye the sight before me was unbelievable for the man seemed to hide all of this from human sight. People walking by would see him strolling and a bird flying overhead not a man fighting a dragon. The man however raised his sword holding tight to the pommel he struck out at the dragon. The dragon gave great fight as I watched in horror the dragon struck at him producing his own sword. Who knew that dragons too fought with swords? The swords clanged the sound resonating in my ears yet no one on the street but me stopped and stared.

The dragon yelled, "I am Odysseus. I am the oldest dragon alive. Do you think to slay me mortal?"

"Know me well Dragon. I am Regulus and I will send thee to thy doom. Odysseus, have you not wondered why your number has dwindled?"

The fight continued the swords tips cutting flesh in both dragon and foe. I grew frightened who would defend us from these unseen foe if not for this hereto unknown Regulus?

With a breath the dragon blew fire. Regulus produced a shield and with a movement not unlike a tango, Regulus danced across and deftly found his target piercing Odysseus' heart ending the dragon's life. Regulus turned to me finger to his lips and disappeared never to be seen by me again; but I know what I saw and I'll never forget the magnificent ***Regulus the dragon slayer!***

May Day

It was Beltane, the first of May but these savages didn't seem to celebrate the coming of summer. She missed the festival, the dancing and the joy of the coming summer. She would have been able to join the dance of fertility this year and pick a husband; instead she was condemned to be a slave by these conquering peoples. There would be no bonfire, no singing, and no feasting, for Tuatha this year. A ship had transported her to foreign land to slavery.

Had she been penalized by the Goddess for her vanity? If so that wasn't just she hadn't been as overly vain as other maidens in her village. She hadn't been generous with herself as others had. She was still a maid and what was her reward? She had been dragged to these strange lands and now served her mistress fetching and carrying and fending off her mistress's lecherous husband Adalbert. She would keep herself pure and escape to her people one day that was her dream.

Home! Would she find any of her peoples there, or would they all be with different tribes, as she was serving their masters? The language of her masters was not one she had totally mastered, having been with them for only a month, she only knew a few words...enough to complete chores and to refuse advances.

How Tuatha missed her sisters and her mother's soft voice as she woke them in the morning. Even her father's scolding would sound good to her right now. She wanted to be in her father's dwelling, but she feared that would never be possible. Tuatha finished preparing her mistress and master's food and placed them on a tray.

Tuatha crept into her mistresses' room with the drink and food. She bent to wake her and found her mistress... dead. She turned to wake her master and found that he too was dead. She trembled with fear lest she be blamed for their deaths .She became more and more afraid, lest she be blamed for the deaths. Granted her mistress and master appeared to be old, most likely she had been sixty years or more on this earth, it could be considered a natural death. However they both died at the same time and the slave was always blamed first, lest they have poisoned their masters. But where could she flee? If she fled they would take it for a sign of her guilt. Surely that would make things worse.

Tuatha knew there was no escape. She raised the alarm, letting them know in sign language her mistress and master were now dead. They nattered on in their language but she didn't understand. She was seized by rough hands, shaken, and then bound. Her hands and feet were wrapped in rope. They placed her in a boat alongside her mistress and master. Then the boat was set ablaze. She should have run she thought.

As the flames grew higher and Tuatha knew there was no escape she closed her eyes. Bidding her life goodbye and she left her body and her spirit travelled to her home Brigantia, but as she looked around she saw nothing but ashes. Brigantia was gone. It had probably been burnt in the same raid they had taken her as a slave. Did that mean her family had been taken prisoner too? Or were they like her now dead?

She felt a tug and a pull as a light appeared before her she followed. There she saw her mother's face, her sisters smiling. She touched her mother's face as her mother smiled again, welcoming Tuatha. Her father was there too. Tuatha was home. They could not steal her soul. Mayday reborn from the ashes; the people reincarnated to live freely again.

~0~

Spell

As a young newly married woman, Amara lay dying; she begged her best friend, Crystal who now held her hand, "Take care of him."

"I will I promise, Amara."

Amara put a small bag in Crystal's hand.

"What is this?"

"It's a counteraction spell. If any evil woman tries to be-spell Andrew blow this in her face and she'll be repelled. I am a druid priestess after all."
Andrew came in and said," Crystal, my beloved's time draws nigh. Will you nae come back later?"

"I will," Crystal answered.

Amara died a short time later. Crystal arranged the funeral and the wake. She cooked and cleaned every day for Andrew looking after him as she promised. A year later Andrew met Delilah and Crystal was pushed aside. Crystal didn't believe in spells or the fact her friend Amara had believed she was a druid priestess, but she had made a promise. Crystal vowed to test Delilah. Delilah failed every test put to her. Delilah was cruel to the waitress, the bellman at Andrew's apartment. She yelled at little children. Andrew couldn't, or would see how mean Delilah was to other people. He seemed to be totally under her spell. Crystal used the counteraction spell and Delilah left never to return.

Andrew looked stunned and bewildered.

"I don't understand...I thought that woman was you," he told Crystal, "You've been there for me since Amara died. It is you who loved us both. Will you marry me?"

"I thought you never ask," Crystal replied.

From up above the clouds parted, Amara smiled; Andrew was safe and would be happy. She could rest now.

Skull Splitter

My head was splitting. Long blonde hair was in my face, and my hair was chocolate brown. Lying beside me, his eyes wide open, was a real life Viking, his helmet on the table beside the bed. Why did I drink Skull Splitter ale last night? It obviously had terrible side effects.

"About last night lass..." the Scottish brogue started.
"Don't fret; you made a mistake now you want to leave," I filled in.
"Nae Aimil."
"Where did you come from? A Viking Scot?"
"Dinnae you mind th' bottle? You saved me frae the bottle."
"You were drinking too much?"
"Nae I was in the bottle!" he insisted.
"Are you telling me you were a Scottish Viking genie in a bottle? Preposterous."
"Is it lass? What kin ah do tae make ye believe me?"
"Can you make me rich with someone who I can love and will love me forever?"
"Ach I did all that last nicht," he said showing me a wedding ring on his finger and one on my mine then kissed me so passionately I could feel it down to my toes.
I was in a nightmare, or was it a dream come true? Surely I had one more wish?

"I wish you'd never leave me."
"Dane."

Spending endless days and nights with my genie, life is magical; but the bottle is a little tight and stuffy. Oh well, we can't have it all can we?

~0~

Spring

"Did you see that Mother?"
"Yes my dear. I saw the sprout. Even the ants are awakening from their long winters nap."
"I still don't understand where will *Winter* go? Is *he* dead?"
"No, my child, *he* will slumber until *he* is needed again. Now do you feel the change?"
"Yes, I feel more alive. What is happening to me?"
"It's almost time for the strange and fantastical happenings in the garden."
"I don't understand *Mother Gaia*."
"You will my dear child, this is your first time as *Spring*."
"*Spring?*"
"Yes my child, now go forth and spread your magic."

~0~

Goddess

P adraig, the brave, sought a goddess who was missing.

He heard that the goddess might have been captured and entombed in the cave of lost souls. He gathered his tools and his mightiest stead and travelled the long treacherous journey to the cave of lost souls. Arriving he entered the cave torch in hand he ventured forward in pitch blackness. His torch snuffed out at the meekest light. The cave echoed and he feared what he might find in the darkness as he heard scurrying sounds like rats or other animals and some other odd sounds he in the distance he just couldn't identify. Feeling his way slowly he realized there was a gaping hole ahead. Something told him in this specific gaping hole, he would find the woman. Had she fell in? Or been placed there so she could not leave?

Padraig threw down rope and climbed into the pit and drew back in surprise. All around him mindless souls wandered in cold and snow. How could it snow in a cave?
Souls in torment with great gnashing of teeth, moans and cries that seemed to echo inside him filled the space. He gathered his courage and called,"Caileach Bheur?"
"I am Caileach, would you kill me now?"
"It is tempting but I have actually come to rescue you."
"You rescue me from this living hell that Blodewedd, Brigit and Ostara have thrown me?"
"It was not they who did this to you. It was Cally Berry."
"Why has she done this to me?"
"Cally has been punished. Spring will not come until May."
"So you free me to cure diseases and bring forth winter?"

"I do."
"Lead me out of this pit so I may take pity on those here and help them out so they might warm by the fire and you take them home."
"But you are winter. You have no pity. "
"You are wrong. I bring them time to share a feast, revel and sing and come together; for as the cold winds cool the earth the earth regenerates and brings forth the hope of spring, "She answered.

Padraig showed Caileach the rope and with his help she helped free the people trapped there and Winter was reborn.

~0~

The Secwécwpemc People

T he boat had landed on the shores of a vast territory.
Everywhere you looked green trees, mountains rising up
from the earth. Not just any trees great fir trees that almost
touch the sky in their beauty. Their lungs could breathe
pure fresh air and their bodies felt alive with the earth. The
men could see why the Hudson Bay Company wanted this
area scouted and the goods that the natives and trappers
could provide brought to them. There were animals in
abundance to trap and the men were to go further into the
wilderness and see what other animals they could trap for
their furs before they reached their destination.

They walked for days over mountains, down mountains
until they came to another beautiful area where the
mountain met a crystal clear lake, fed by mountain streams.
One of the first scouts to the area had divulged the first time
Henry had visited that there was godless, native peoples
living here. But Henry Waller knew there could not be
anyone godless in beauty like this.

He had welcomed the chance to trade with the Secwepemc
or Shuswap tribe nomadic peoples who lived in this area in
the summer for trading. Now with the Hudson Bay
Company monopoly ending even more traders would be
entering these formerly insignificant wilderness areas to
trap and trade goods with other companies. They then
would import these goods to Europe and other places furs,
and dried animal parts. Henry knew his contact with these
indigenous peoples would help him and his men to come
out ahead of the trading wars that might come.

When Henry had met the tribe three years he had been welcomed the chief himself, Apenimon and met his daughter Aponi who was betrothed to Askuwheteau. His son Bemossed had not been so welcoming and had challenged Henry to fishing and hunting that Henry had excelled at. Henry had allowed Bemossed to beat him, only to keep Bemossed's pride, but Bemossed had guessed that Henry had done so. Bemossed appreciated the gesture, since he as chief's son was expected to be the best. Henry and Bemossed had become friends and thus Henry stayed for over a year with the tribe collecting pelts and dried body parts to sell to the Hudson Bay Company.

Their language very difficult to understand but Henry strived to master it. Living with the tribe for over a year, Henry learned more than simple phrases, he could now understand and speak their language. Though phrases like Secwécwpemc - ken ri7 which meant I am Shuswap the name of their tribe and Weyt-k which meant Hello if you spoke to more than one you said Weyt-kp, he taught to his men. The tribe wanted him to stay and were disappointed when he left. He hoped they would welcome him and his men warmly again.

Henry and his men entered the grounds of the tribe to find them ailing, many were coughing droplets that flew through the air and landed on the men. Smallpox decimated the once large tribe. All around him people were suffering or dying. He found Askuwheteau dead and Aponi shivering over his body. Bemossed could not be found.

Henry had suffered and survived from smallpox when he was five so he had immunity from the disease, Henry began administering to the sick and dying. His men fled into the forest away from the sickness lest they too be inflicted with smallpox. Some came back ill and trembling and Henry worked night and day ministering to all of the sick with some of the tribes' unaffected women. When the sickness started to pass some seven days later, and the bodies were counted, the dead numbered over two hundred more of the tribe dead and all of Henry's men that had come back from the forest.

Henry began bury the bodies and found the rest of his own men dead at the edge of the woods. They too had succumbed to the disease. Henry felt bad that traders had brought this illness to the people he grown to respect and admire.

The chief survived and rewarded Henry with membership in the tribe. Henry decided that this was the life he wanted and he joined the tribe. A year later Aponi became his wife and they settled into a good life. Henry fished and hunted in the good months and they had food to feed the members of the tribe. They grew crops and were self-sufficient. They had six sons and one daughter who lived a full life.
The tribe continued to foster and grow until the colonial government divided the Secwepemc people into seventeen distinct groups with specific parcels of land designated to each. The Secwepemc people he was with stayed in the area of the lake and continued the old ways, but it wasn't the same. Henry knew that with the land grab of the colonial government more couldn't be far behind. Henry and Aponi's descendants now still live in Kamloops not far from Shuswap Lake. As Henry suspected the land was taken from them however the old stories are told from generation to generation in the Heritage Park where the tribes' history is told today.

~0~

Child of The Cuckoo's Nest

The mother toiled long and hard, bringing the child into the world. The child that was born was handsome, his hair, curly blonde and tight, to his little head. The mother cooed over him and her husband Olaf was proud to call him son.

The other women in the small village fawned over him and envied the woman Emelie. Her husband gave her riches and now he gave her a son? Not any son either; but a baby with winsome smile and blue eyes that gleamed like diamonds. It was not fair they claimed… she had everything.

Emelie bathed in the adulation. She had given birth to a child all adored. She would wait until her husband Olaf slept and then creep into the nursery. Emelie loved to look at the baby, when all were asleep. It was their quiet time just mother and son to be together. She would suckle him at his breast, as she talked to him of all he would accomplish and he would look up at her with his big blue eyes, gurgling.

One night Emilie heard a noise in the nursery as her husband lay beside her trying to go to sleep. Emelie dismissed the noise, even as her breast dampened with the milk waiting to be suckled. Her husband bid her go in and check on the child. When she went into Marcus she thought he looked different somehow but dismissed the idea as preposterous. She got him to lie down and went back into her husband missing her chance to be with her boy that night.

The boy grew and his mother Emelie wondered why he did not walk yet, or talk yet. He could not feed himself and he would not be trained to not wear diapers. He certainly didn't speak. What had happened to the boy? Then she remembered the noise when he was a baby. Could someone have stolen her child and replaced him with this broken child? Had she been too proud of her son? Emelie thought of how foolish this was. This was her child there was no doubt not in her heart. Even if it was not she would fight to keep this boy. She loved him.

The boy Marcus was slow to walk, finally walking at four years of age, but by then others were noticing, how truly different he was. He could play a harpsichord and sing beautiful pieces and yet he spoke, no word he did not sing.

If his father's accounting books were put before him, even at four years of age; he was able to compute all the sums to totals, faster than any normal full grown man could. He read books in his father's library beyond his years and yet he did not speak. Others in the small village were afraid of him because he wouldn't speak or look them directly in the eye. Marcus screamed and trembled, an unholy noise was heard when he was touched. Emelie was careful to protect him and make sure no person touched him but she worried that she had not done enough for the child.

Olaf's heart grew cold towards the boy. He found him annoying. He didn't hesitate to tell Emelie that he wondered where this child had come from. He began at first to suggest Emelie must have broken their marriage vows to conceive Marcus. Emilie was a good wife to Olaf and she protested that this was not possible begging him to love the child, but Olaf saw only failure in the child and he would not. Finally Marcus told Emelie it was obvious to him that the noise that they heard in the nursery, was a fairy placing her child in Marcus' place.

Emelie tried to convince him otherwise, but Olaf wouldn't budge. He began to treat the child as if he was a stranger. Emelie grew angry with him and her heart hardened against Olaf, to the point where she kept him from her bed. Finally Olaf left her obtaining an annulment from the priest citing the defective child, as he called Marcus.

Emelie struggled to feed herself and her child. She took jobs cleaning homes of those who took pity on she who had once been the lady of the village. They even allowed her to bring Marcus.

Meanwhile Olaf married another woman in the village. She was pregnant with his son. Carl. Carl was spoiled by Olaf. Olaf said he was grateful now to have a normal child and not one from the cuckoo's nest. He tried to sour the village against Marcus, but Marcus' good deeds fixing things that others could not made him well liked in the village.

Marcus learned to speak and was soon speaking the languages that traders brought to the village. Emelie still protected her son he was her world and she did all she could to make him succeed. She sought books from traders spending any spare monies to obtain them for Marcus. These books opened worlds of knowledge for Marcus. Emelie could see that Marcus learned much from them as he began repairing things he found broken and talking of things she'd never heard, or dreamed of.

When her employers well stopped working, Marcus at twelve years of age, conceived a way for it to work again. Marcus was ingenious; solving problems in the village that even grown man could not. He grew older and Emelie continued to watch over and protect her son.

When Marcus was a mere twenty, the King who had heard of his brilliance begged him to come to his court to solve a problem of great secrecy. None in the village were to know where he went. Marcus however told his mother of the strongly worded request. Emelie was afraid for her son.

There were many people at the King's court and Marcus did not do well with people. Emelie convinced the King's messenger that she was necessary for Marcus to complete his task and she was able to go with him.

When they went with the messenger all in the village thought the King was punishing them. Olaf was glad. His boy Carl now sixteen, could now succeed without being compared to the cuckoo in the nest Marcus. There were those in the village that rejoiced that the man who made them so uncomfortable was gone. They rejoiced and said a curse was lifted. Others in the village were frightened who now would fix what couldn't be fixed if Marcus wasn't there? Marcus was a saviour of their village why couldn't they see how they had prospered since he started fixing problems in the village?

Emelie was just worried about how to protect her son in the King's court. Marcus was excited about the books he would be able to read there and did not seem to understand how many people might be there. She would protect her son as she always had he would be safe in this world. She would make it so.

~0~

Marcus had never been in along carriage ride before and he didn't feel well with the constant rocking of the coach. He moaned then he cried loudly then he rocked himself back and forth. Emelie was worried the last time Marcus had acted this way he made himself so sick he was sick for two weeks. He didn't eat he didn't sleep and Emelie had feared for his life. The doctor had drugged Marcus and he had slept.

Emelie tried to comfort Marcus now in the carriage but he would not be comforted. Instead it was like he was juggling everything in the carriage and not catching any of it. It was then she resorted to her last measure, she did what she had sworn she'd never do to Marcus, she drugged him with laudanum again as the doctor had done. Marcus slept the two days it took them to get to the palace. When they arrived they will spirited through a back door of the palace.

Emelie worried about all the secrecy. People could disappear this way. This could be a ploy just to rid the all of their presence, she only hoped it wouldn't be. They would fawn over the King and perhaps that would protect them.

"King Eric will see you soon Lady Bjelbo, Master Magnusson."
"My son is fully grown and therefore must be addressed as the honourable Marcus Magnusson, as my father is Jarl," rebuked Emilie.
"If your father is Jarl, why do you struggle to live?" the servant asked.
"I make my own way, my father makes his," Marcus muttered softly, surprising his mother.
"Very well mistress, you can explain this to King Eric," The servant replied leaving.

Looking around the large room Emilie was surprised to find a table that had an engine and some small parts. Marcus noticed it at the same time and wandered over to it. Once there his dexterous fingers began placing the small parts into the machine within a few minutes all the parts were in the machine and he was able to fix the small cuckoo clock.

A man limped into the room on his good leg and navigated straight to the cuckoo clock. He was dressed in fine clothes and followed closely by the servant. The limping man examined the cuckoo clock and smiled.

"Lady Bjelbo, honourable Marcus Magnusson?" asked King Eric.

Emilie dropped into a deep curtsey and made Marcus bow beside her.

"Yes, sire," Emilie answered raising her head and smiling, a little but Marcus just nodded his head still bowed.
"Does your son, not speak Lady Bjelbo?"
"I speak when it is necessary, but mother speaks for me."
"Your son is indeed as different as I had heard, but unlike I had perceived he is not addlepated," King Eric stated.
"My son is not addlepated. How dare they?" and then blanching as Emilie realized that she had said something harshly to her King as if she was his contemporary, Emilie exclaimed, "Forgive me sire."
"I understand the need to protest, my dear. The usurper sought to use my difference against me. He succeeded for three years but I prevailed," King Eric explained indicating his left leg shorter than the other.

His aid gasped at the King's frankness.

"Sire, we rejoiced when the true King, yourself reigned again,"Emelie waxed.

"Of course you did. You are my subjects."

"Yes, they are sire and you need not concern yourself with this duty. I can handle this for you," whispered the King's servant.

"Quiet Ander, when I want your opinion I will ask for it," King Eric.

"Sire, I am so sorry. I overstepped my bounds."

"Leave now, Anders .Wait, outside the doors."

"But sire."

"I am not in any danger," King Eric exclaimed angrily, "You will leave now."

The King's aide then left the room closing the doors.

"You passed my test by fixing my cuckoo clock. Marcus I have a great task for you. Perhaps it is a simple task for you. Perhaps not! But I am hoping that you are up to the task. None of my advisors, nor my Uncle's advisors have been unable to uncover the culprit."

"Culprit?" Emilie asked.

"Do you speak for your son? I realize you have protected the boy for all time but he is now a man, give him time to answer for himself," rebuked King Eric.

"Have I done this Marcus?" Emilie asked, "Have I kept you from your manhood?"

"Mother you have spoken for me, but I was willing," Marcus answered.

Emilie was worried had she tried to so much for Marcus that she had not allowed him to be the man he so obviously was? She would try hard to give him his freedom and treat him as his age while still protecting him.

"What would you have me do, Sire?" Marcus retorted in a quiet respectful voice.

"I have a troubling problem, that I think you can solve."

"Me?" Marcus answered.

"Yes, young man, I think you can or you wouldn't be here."

"What if my son cannot achieve this?"

"Marcus, I ask much of you, but as your King, I demand you try hard to solve this. Your country needs this as much."

"I'll try, Sire."

"That is all I ask."

"The problem?"

"I have a number of tasks for you. The most urgent, someone is stealing monies from my coffers. The ledgers appear to have no money missing, but I know for myself that I had more money than the books show. That money was set aside for helping the people with their needs and now someone has stolen from your King. I don't know how they have done so never the less the money is missing. I understand you have great skill with numbers as well as your abilities to fix things. I would have you find the discrepancy so I can name the culprit. "

"Where is the book?"

"Here and a pen and ink," King Eric responded, "If you succeed there will be great reward."

Marcus began reading the ledger immediately. He was so obsessed with the ledger he did not see the King leave.

Emelie watched and waited. She knew what happened when Marcus became obsessed he would not eat or drink until he found what the King needed. She only hoped he would find it.

Two hours later Marcus closed the book. Emelie knew that Marcus had done what the King's advisors had not found the discrepancy. She must protect him until he told the King.

~0~

E/melie continued to be worried about Marcus. She felt

the need to caution Marcus about his find, when he confessed he had found the hidden discrepancies. She felt she must sear this knowledge into his brain, to trust no one, but the King.

"Marcus dear you must share this information with no one but the King."
"But mother, I found the information shouldn't everyone know?" asked Marcus proudly.
"My son, there are some things people will harm you for. Do you remember the children in the village who would kick you and hit you when you were young?"
"I remember they put bruises on my flesh."
"There are people like that here. Whoever has taken the King's gold, does not want to be discovered. They are not novices they have been stealing probably for a long time."
"I don't understand. Why would someone do that?"
"Marcus dear, do we have much money?"
"No, mother."
"Do you remember when you asked me for the parts to make your equipment?"
"Yes, but you said we didn't have the money for it."
"Exactly some people who do not have enough money take it."
"Like the person who took the King's gold? But that is wrong and they should be punished."
"Yes my son but not everyone thinks as we do. This person will not want to be caught, for they fear the punishment. So you must not tell none but the King, that you have discovered the trick of how the money went missing."
"Very well Mother, but if I am asked what should I say?"
"The first time you are asked say I am working, but I cannot find this problem yet."
"And if they ask again what will I say?"

"Tell them the problem is vexing and that even with your genius it is difficult."
"But it isn't mother," Marcus protested.
"I know but they won't."
"I will do this."

Their conversation was interrupted as the doors to the room opened and an unknown person came into the room. He was followed by a servant carrying food and drinks, who set the food down on the table then promptly left.

Emelie stared at the man who had entered with the servant. He seemed familiar but she knew no one at court. His hair was dark almost black his eyes were a most peculiar dark brown almost black.

Emelie began to worry, this man had entered without the King and had now dismissed the servant. Why would he do that? His gaze when he looked at Marcus was one of suspicion put Emelie even more on edge.

Marcus pretended to work on the problem staring at the ledger and turning the pages to Emelie's relief. Marcus even answered the questions the man asked in the correct manner. Emelie breathed a sigh of relief.
"Wouldn't you like to take and have some tea? The servant has brought some cakes and drink," the man offered.

Emelie wanted to refuse but she knew they were both thirsty and hungry. She took the offered cup and drank it down. Marcus was more hesitant and continued ignoring the man as if he was examining the ledgers.

"Don't drink or eat anything Marcus," Emelie managed to say as she felt into a faint.

As she drifted under she heard Marcus' painful wails of 'Mother." and the rocking he did when he was upset. She wanted to wake up and help him, but it seemed it was impossible as she was taken further under and into unconsciousness.

~0~

Marcus began the exercise. His mother had taught him to calm himself. He counted over and over to twenty. The man who had harmed his mother shook Marcus, but Marcus continued counting calming himself to defeat the man he now thought of as a monster.

"Marcus calm yourself .Can you not see I wish you no harm?"
"I do not know you. YOU HARMED MY MOTHER! 654321879!" Marcus yelled.
"She is unharmed, she but sleeps. I would not harm one hair on her head. She is your mother and once upon a time I had feelings for her."
"You loved my Mother? Then why did you harm her?" asked Marcus puzzled.
"Marcus you wound me. I am your uncle Ragnor. Your Father Olaf. is a fool. He has made a huge error in judgement. He set you his greatest treasure aside. I would not have done so. I told your father he was being a fool; that you were his son, the fruit of his looms and therefore you would show your worth. Lo and behold I was vindicated your worth has been shown, the King himself brought you here."
Marcus was not swayed by what this man might say. He claimed he was his Uncle but if he wasn't anything like his brother, (Marcus' Father) Olaf, he was not a good man. His father had kicked him in the street when he was but a small boy. His mother was asleep, his Uncle claimed, but she did not wake. What if she never woke? Marcus just glared at the man.

The man grew angry at Marcus continued his defiance.

"I wish you to help me, for has not your mother taught you to help family?" the monster asked.

Marcus next thought was of escape but how with his mother like this, he could not take her with him. She would not leave him, he could not leave her.

Marcus' thoughts were interrupted by the rooms' only door opening and two men entering the room.

"Tis past your time. Where have you been?" asked the monster, he now knew as his Uncle Ragnor.
"Sorry Master, we did not want the King to see us."
"Help with this man, but handle him gently he is valuable,"Ragnor demanded.
"Master shall we dispose of the woman's body?"

Marcus let out a gasp of air, that he didn't even know he had been holding, at hearing this. Surely his Uncle needed his mother if only for his cooperation in whatever he wanted and they would be safe?

"Give him the tea, than we will handle the woman."
"Master?"
"The tea is drugged. The woman is not dead but sleeping. Now do as I have ordered. Hold him down and pour the tea down his throat." Then turning to Marcus, Ragnor explained, sounding regretful, "I am sorry it has to be this way Marcus but when you get to know me, I'm sure you'll see I'm doing this to protect you. If the King found out your worth, he'd keep you forever imprisoned."

Uncle Ragnor wanted him to drink the tea? But mother said do not drink the tea. Marcus wasn't fooled he didn't trust this man no matter how much he tried to be nice. His Uncle was forcing him to drink the tea.

Marcus readied himself to fight back but the men were big. The two men combined, weighed as much as four men his size. He was unable to stop them, try as he might, from pouring the tea down his throat. In a few minutes he became tired. He prayed they wouldn't harm his mother and they would both be safe, as the men still held him waiting for something.

As he drifted off to sleep, he felt the men's grips lessen and he heard a jingle sounding like keys being taken out of a pocket.

"Pick up the boy and the woman but don't forget the book. The King must never know my crime. Take them to the hut and keep them there until I come. I must appear blameless in this crime and the King must see my grief at the disappearance of my nephew.

"So you want us to kill him?" asked one of the men.

"No, I have other plans for him," Ragnor replied, "Remember the princely sum you receive for this and do not betray me or you will regret it."

~0~

M arcus woke up, his head heavy from the tea he had been forced to drink. He glanced around noting that the hut his Uncle Ragnor had spoken of seemed to be a hunting lodge. He spotted his mother Emelie lying on a bench with a thin blanket and placed a small cushion under her head so she was comfortable. Why was she still asleep? Had his Uncle Ragnor really told the truth and she wasn't dying?

Marcus felt beneath her nose for air escaping her mouth and listened to her breath. Then he put his head on her chest to check her heartbeats. Her heartbeats were steady, she was alive, but why did she not wake?

Where were the men that had brought them here to this building? Should he worry about them or could he somehow lift his mother in her weakened state and escape? The two men were guarding the front door he noticed. If Mother was awake, they could leave out the window at the back no one was guarding it.

"Mother wake up we are in danger," Marcus demanded shaking his mother.
"Marcus I'm tired let me sleep just a little longer."
"Mother you have to wake up. We are in danger."
"Danger? Where are we?" his mother asked, waking up enough to know something was wrong.
"We've been drugged and kidnapped. We have to escape."
"I have to wake up."
"Yes mother."
"You'll have to help me. I'm so tired."
"I can do this mother."
"I know you can," Emelie agreed.

Marcus helped his mother through the window and they fled into the forest behind the hunting lodge. Marcus kept searching behind them for the men. Just when Marcus thought they had gotten away without being followed he heard their loud thunder feet behind him. Up ahead he saw a clearing it seemed there was nowhere to hide.

"Are you fleeing those men?" a voice from nowhere said. Marcus didn't answer. He was busy trying to find a place to hide. Marcus worried his mother was near collapse, as she tittered back and forth barely standing.

"I'm speaking to you. Will you not answer me? I could help you'd if you listen."

Marcus looked up and saw a woman hiding in the tree. Her hair was the colour of the midnight sky. Her eyes were a warm brown that sparkled when she spoke and her mouth curled into a welcoming smile. She was tiny barely five feet tall, but Marcus felt strength in her he'd seen only in one other woman, his mother.

"Come, I know a secret tunnel nearby where they can't find you." She claimed, "A mist is coming it will cover the entrance and hide you from their gaze."
"Why were you up in the tree?" asked Marcus curiously.
"How else can I see what is going on in the world?" she responded.

Marcus was amazed and captivated by this woman. She was like no young woman he'd ever met. She scampered down from the tree and he noticed that she had tucked her bulky dress into her pantaloons .He blushed and looked away as she adjusted her clothing.

"I am Lady Ingrid Jägerhon, who are you?"

A lady in a tree. Just how old was Lady Jägerhon? Marcus wondered. She appeared to be about twenty or possible twenty two years of age. Was she married?

"I am Lord Marcus Magnusson and this is my mother, Lady Emelie Bjelbo.do you live nearby?"
"Yes, I live nearby with my guardian. She doesn't look well is your mother ailing?"
"Those men drugged and kidnapped us. I fear my mother is still under the influence of the drugged tea."
"But you said your name was Marcus Magnusson. Are you not under the King's protection? Why would his guards kidnap you?"
"Can we discuss this when we reach the cave and are well hidden from these men?"
"Very well, Lord Magnusson, come quickly I hear their footsteps."

Marcus ran ahead, his mother slung over his shoulder.

"Hey slow down so I can show you which way to go in the cave."
"Okay, then go to the left and hide way back. I'll be back in a few minutes," Ingrid instructed.

It was damp and slimy in the cave and Marcus worried what the cold would due to his mother. Marcus crouched resigned to stay in the cave until they were safe. Shielding his mother and keeping her warm in a dark corner of the cave, Marcus heard the muffled voices of the men and Ingrid speaking. When Ingrid didn't come back right away worried for her safety. Maybe he should have made her stay in the cave with them?

A few minutes later he heard, "Marcus? Marcus it's safe it's me, Ingrid."

Marcus decided not to answer suddenly worried that Ingrid was in conspiracy with the two men. How else had she gotten away from them so easily?

He heard her creep down the tunnel and got ready to hit her over the head if necessary to protect himself and his mother.

He pulled himself back from throwing the blow as he realized it was Ingrid. Surely she had an explanation for fraternizing he'd hear her out first.

"What are you doing? That hurt me. You were trying to clobber me over the head. Why?" asked Ingrid, sounding like Marcus hurt her feelings.
"You were talking to those men," Marcus replied.
"Of course I was talking to those men. Number one, they're my cousins and it would be suspicious if I didn't speak to the big louts. Two, I told them I saw a man and a woman go in the opposite direction."
"They are your cousins?"
"That is what I said. I really don't like them much though. They are very thick headed and low browed. If someone asks them to do something as long as they are paid they do it. They don't even think about it. I don't know why the King hasn't caught on to the fact, that they are not fit to work for him," rambled Ingrid.
"But should you not be loyal to them because they are family?" Marcus asked.

"Are you loyal to your other family? These two have made my life miserable. I can't count the number of beatings I got because they tattled, or made things up to my governess."
"Those men kidnapped me and my mother on behalf of my Uncle Ragnor, so no I am not loyal to him. I was looking at the King's books and I found the discrepancies that would have had him punished by the King."

"You need to hide until we can get you to the King. Your Uncle Ragnor is very powerful and he won't easily let you get to the King with this information. It could mean his death."

"Can't you tell the King? You said you were his ward," Marcus asked.

"No. Being his ward means only his protection. I do not see the King very often. I see him only when he summons me. Perhaps you should hide out here."

"This cave is damp and cold. I don't think this is a good place for my Mother," Marcus complained

"Let me see her."

Ingrid then went to Emilie's side and checked her breathing and placed her head on her chest.

"She breathes still but her breath is shallow. You are correct this cave and its dampness aren't good for her. I think they gave her too much of whatever they drugged her with."

"Do you think she'll wake soon?" Marcus asked.

"I think it is in God's hands; but I believe she is a strong woman and will come back to you," Ingrid stated confidently.

"How do you know she's strong? You don't know her," Marcus complained.

"I've met her son and he seems strong and capable. Only a strong woman could have raised a son like that by herself. Come now I know a secret entrance into the castle and a room no one ever goes into that you could hide."

"Hide in the castle? Isn't that dangerous?" Marcus demanded.

"It's the last place they would look for you and once your mother is recovered you can go to the King and tell him all." Ingrid explained. "Your Uncle has many allies though in the castle, maybe it would better for me to ask for an audience with the King then tell him all and then bring the King to you."

"You do this for us? Why?"

'Because it's the right thing to do," Ingrid explained.

"Thank-you," Marcus said quietly.

"Come now, once they don't find you they will be back and look here," Ingrid explained.

"I hear something, I think they've doubled back," Marcus exclaimed.

"If they find me with you, I will be severely punished or they might kill us all," Ingrid said clinging to Marcus.

After a few minutes and seeing no one Marcus mind began to wander. Marcus thought of Ingrid's age and wondered if she was taken? He had never before liked it when someone touched him, but Ingrid's touch was light and he felt like he wanted her to continue to touch him.

He felt the need to protect her and keep her safe. Was this the love of which mother spoke of? Could she be the one, he was told to wait for? What was he thinking? A woman like that would never be interested in a man like him... would she? Marcus glanced over at her again and missed a woman and her cart going by the cave entrance. Marcus suddenly realized Ingrid had murmured something to him.

"It's safe to go now Marcus. Marcus are you listening to me? You are looking at me so funny."

"Sorry it is the effects of the drugs," Marcus lied and followed Ingrid who carried his mother.

Ingrid led Marcus to the back of the castle. Tapping on a wall she struggled for a moment, pulling at something he couldn't see and he was surprised to see a door pop out.

"Come on we need to hurry and keep quiet so no one hears us in the passageway. The guards who patrol here will come around that corner soon," Ingrid demanded pushing Marcus through the door and shutting the door quickly.

Marcus looked around. It was pitch black and he couldn't see two feet in front of him. It was worse than the fog which had seemed to linger outside the cave. Ingrid however, appeared to see like a cat in the dark. Marcus followed her down what looked to be a tunnel or a corridor. Carrying his mother was becoming difficult as his arms groaned; tired from the unaccustomed weight Marcus started to wonder if this winding corridor would ever end when Ingrid suddenly came to an abrupt stop.
"We're here. Let me check the hallway to make sure no one is there and then we can go to the storage room."

It seemed longer than the ten minutes, it took her to check the corridor and Marcus began to worry she had been captured. He'd set his mother down and checked on her. She was still breathing softly and seemed at peace.

"What took you so long?" Marcus asked Ingrid when she reappeared.
"There was someone in the corridor. I had to explain myself."
"Did you make them go away?" Marcus demanded.
"Of course I did, silly."
"What did you say?"
"I told them in my most aristocratic manner, that they had no business here."

Marcus gave Ingrid a look she misinterpreted for disapproval.

"What do you think I was too lenient with them? Should I call them back?" Ingrid asked sarcastically.
"Can we go to the room now?" Marcus asked trying to change the subject.

Marcus sensed that Ingrid was annoyed, but didn't understand why.

"Yes, but hurry I don't want to have to explain myself to anyone else."

Marcus entered the hallway and the light blinded him after being in the dark so long. He stumbled slightly almost dropping his mother. He caught himself, bending down on one knee and balancing the weight of his mother in his arms.

"Are you okay? Don't worry it's not much further."
"That is good, because Mother needs to lie down," Marcus commented.

Ingrid knocked on a wall. A brick was turned and then a handle popped out of the wall. Ingrid seized the handle and a magically a door appeared out of the wall. Frankly Marcus was amazed at the craftsmanship it took to build such a hidden door. Then he started to worry, obviously someone knew the door was here and had built it for some reason. What were the chances of them finding Marcus and his mother before Ingrid could go to the King?

"Don't worry Marcus I will keep you both safe," Ingrid cried. Then putting a finger to her mouth she whispered, "Hush, someone comes."
"Ingrid what are you doing here?" asked a voice, a few minutes later.

Marcus was amazed, how did Ingrid hear someone coming when he didn't?

"Hello Hakan."
"You've found them? Good work Ingrid, the King will be pleased."

"Hakan I must tell the King myself, until then they must stay hidden here. Someone close to him kidnapped them to prevent him from finding out what they had done. If I do not tell the King myself well then..."

"You've seen what will happen? It is bad?"

"Yes Hakan. It would be very bad. You know I have seen our future as well."

"We will be together, but you had to wait for the King's approval first," Hakan remembered.

"Then you will do this for me?"

"I don't know Ingrid. The King might be unhappy with me, should I do so."

"Hakan, I thought you loved me. If you can't do this simple thing for me and the good of the kingdom..."

"I am sorry Ingrid. I do love you. I will give you two days, and then I will go to the King."

"Thank you Hakan," Ingrid replied kissing him on the cheek and then ushered them into the room.

Marcus lay his mother down on the floor and when he turned he noticed that Hakan had not come into the room. Ingrid smiled and then exclaimed..., "I must go now, but I will be back soon with supplies for you and your mother Lord Magnusson."

The door was then closed and Marcus heard a scrapping like a lock being placed across the door. Marcus began to think he was wrong about Ingrid. She had not addressed him as Marcus either but called him Lord Magnusson, like he was a stranger. She was betrothed to Hakan. Why? He seemed from his voice to be a big lout. Why would Ingrid marry Hakan? Was she being forced to by the King? Ingrid had locked them in though, they were trapped. Should Marcus trust her? Was she just placating Hakan, or was he really her true love?

Hakan spoke like Ingrid was a soothsayer. Yet if Ingrid was soothsayer should he not trust her? Would she not see that he, Marcus would strive to make her happy should she pick him?"

"Marcus, where are we?" asked Emilie." I was awake when you brought me in with those people."
"Mother?" Marcus asked, examining her face to see if she was truly awake.
"Where are we Marcus?" Emilie demanded again.
"We are back in the palace but we are in a secret room."
"Back in the palace? Ragnor...Ragnor drugged me with tea. Did you drink Marcus?"
"Yes, he had two men pour it down my throat and then he took us to a hunting lodge in the woods."
"Then how did we get here?"
"I escaped and took you with me. Then I met Lady Ingrid Jägerhon she showed me the way here."
"Lady Jägerhon the King's ward? The woman I saw was she? Then we are safe. We will wait and then go tell the King what you know of the books and Ragnor's treachery."
"Yes, we are safe and yes, mother that is who she said she was."
"She is a woman renowned throughout the Kingdom."
"For what mother?"
"She is a soothsayer. The King often uses her to guide his course."
"I thought she was the one at first mother, but I believe now I was mistaken."
"The one my son?"
"The one you spoke of whose touch I would welcome and who would dwell in my heart."
"This woman touched you and you didn't cringe?"
"No, her touch was light like a butterfly and she has a smile that lights up the sky."
"She has taken your heart Marcus."

"She may have my heart but I do not have hers. She is betrothed to Haken and they have locked us in here."

"Marcus, I saw the glance she gave you and the smile she sent you before leaving. If she is truly a soothsayer, then she will see that Haken would not make an intelligent woman like her happy. She will choose you Marcus if you let her know you are interested."

"Interested?"

"Yes, smile back at her. Touch her hand, things like that," Emilie instructed.

"You are a woman in a million mother! We are locked in a room and you not only reassure me we are safe, but you encourage me to capture the heart of the woman I love."

"You are my son and my world; but if this woman will make you happy and be your life partner I will do everything in my power to make her see you are the one for her."

"Thank you Mother."

"Now tell me more of the woman who will be my daughter," Emilie implored.

Marcus waxed about Ingrid and Emelie listened patiently nodding every once in a while and smiling at her son's obvious infatuation. Emilie hoped and prayed that Ingrid was as good a person as Marcus thought. Marcus always wanted to see the good in people. His sweet gentle heart could be betrayed by those who took advantage.

Emilie was worrying about that heart in a way she too had betrayed that gentle heart. There was something, she had always kept from Marcus. If she hadn't believed he would be harmed by the knowledge, that she would have told him long ago, but she was beginning to think Marcus needed to know her secret to protect himself. After all it really wasn't just her secret to keep.

~0~

Emilie watched Marcus sleep knowing that when he awoke, she must tell her son the secret. Maybe she was staring too hard for in the next instance he awoke.

"Mother, what's wrong? Is someone outside?" Marcus asked coming fully awake.
"No my beloved son, but there is something I must tell you. A secret I have held long to protect myself and you."
"I don't understand Mother."
"Then I will explain my son. When I was a young girl my family who was rich travelled to a home that was in the country."
"We are not rich," Marcus protested.
"I am speaking of my birth family, the family of my mother and father. They may still go to that home I do not know."
"But I thought they were dead?"
"They are dead to me," Emilie replied.
"Did they harm you Mother?"
"They turned me away when I needed help when Olaf threw me out. So they are dead to me."
"So that is your secret, that your parents are alive? I knew that Mother."
"No, Marcus be silent and do not hamper me from telling you the story. As I have told you when I was young only nine, I met a boy. I was not supposed to wander away from the country home, without my nanny or a maid, but I loved to climb trees. I was up a tree and a man came along. He was scary and grabbed me from the tree. He was hurting me and I screamed out and a boy came out of nowhere and pulverized him. He was strong brave and he chased him off. The boy captured my heart."
"I'm glad you were saved. Ingrid was up a tree and in a way she saved us," Marcus commented.

"I guess Ingrid did; but back to my story. The boy was visiting nearby. We talked and laughed and had fun. He came every day of that summer and I snuck out to meet him. We played swords with wooden sticks and he taught me how to fence. He took me to a nearby fall, where we watched the animals saunter through. Why I even saw fawns with their mother," Emilie explained her eyes glowing and her face turning up in a smile.

"That would be nice to have a childhood companion," Marcus commented wistfully.

"You don't seem to grasp what I'm telling you. He was the boy I hoped to someday marry, even at nine years old. He loved me too, he pledged to marry me. One day while he was riding his horse to come to me, the horse stumbled falling and taking him with the horse to the ground. His left leg lay beneath the horse twisted and mangled. I went and got help and that is when I learned who he really was.

"Who was he mother?"

"I told you he hurt his leg. Have you met anyone who limps?"

"Mother, it can't be!" Marcus answered shocked.

"But it is my son. My father was furious with me for putting the monarch at risk and punished me. I didn't see King Eric for a long time after that .King Eric was spirited away by his family to protect him from his cousin, who took the crown from Eric."

"Did you know where he was?"

"No, his name was not to be spoken in society. When it was it was in quiet corners and only rumours were heard, that he had been killed."

"But he wasn't mother we've seen him."

"No, he wasn't killed. I grew up while he was gone. My family introduced me to Olaf, who they wanted to be my husband. I didn't want to agree to marry Olaf, but I wanted a child and a home of my own and Eric was long gone. Two months before my wedding to Olaf my family stayed at our country home. I went for a ride on my horse and stopped to climb a tree. That is where King Eric found me.

"Eric with his advisor was trying to get his throne back. Eric had snuck away from his guards to have some time to himself. We talked. He told me of his life in Norway and what had happened to him, in his other cousin's court. We talked, we laughed and it was like I was nine years old again. Eric said he loved me and wanted to marry me. He would abdicate for good for me. I protested but he said if he couldn't be with me, he didn't want to live. He took my hand threw me up on the back of his horse and took me to a priest, where we were married. We spent three glorious weeks together, until Eric grew cold his guards found him and he, King Eric repudiated me. He taunted me saying he had only been dallying with a foolish girl," Emilie cried here wiping away tears.

"What a foolish man, mother, to choose a throne over a jewel like you."

"Thank you my son but there is more. He treated me as a lady of the night who had lain with him for his money. He said that our marriage was not legal, that he had hired a man to pose as a priest and then he had his guards take me back to my family. But I know it was legal. I have kept the papers all these years. Never you fear."

"I don't understand how he could do that to you. When we saw him the other day, he didn't even appear to know you. Are you sure it was King Eric?"

"It was King Eric, Marcus. Once more, although I didn't realize it at the time, I believe he was lying, pushing me away to try to protect me from his cousin."

"Then why didn't you get back together? Is he angry because you married Father? Is that why he pretended not to know you?"

"I don't know why he didn't seem to recognize me the
other day. At the time he dumped me, I was a young girl
with no financial support. I was sent home to my family and
they were so angry. Father was worried that Olaf wouldn't
marry soiled goods. He yelled at me and said he was
ashamed of me. He had told Olaf that I had been sick the
last two months and he forbid me to tell him the truth. I
remember the conversation with my parents like it was
yesterday...

*"You will marry Olaf as scheduled on Saturday," my father
demanded.*

*"I cannot Father. I am already married before God, to
King Eric."*

*"You are a foolish child and you have done your duty to
your King. He sent you home because he was done with
you. He doesn't love you. You are no longer a maid do you
think any other man will marry you? Besides it was he, who
chose your husband Olaf," Father explained.*

"I am married," I insisted

*"You are not but you will be that child you carry will have
a father on paper. You will not disgrace your family. You
will stay with your family, when it is your time and when
the child comes, we will tell your husband two months
later," my mother explained.*

"My husband will come," I continue to insist.

"Lock her in her room Anise," My father told my mother.

*"I protested. I wanted to refuse to eat, but I was so hungry.
I ate and I slept and wept crying for King Eric locked in my
room. Saturday came and they dressed me in a fine dress. I
was sure King Eric would come but he didn't appear. I
stood before the altar and the priest."*

*"I thought not saying a word would not make me married
but the priest pronounced us husband and wife. I lived as
Olaf's wife until he put me aside and I didn't see King Eric
again until the other day."*

"But it if you did not say the words how could you be
married to my Father?"

"Marcus you haven't listened I was married to your father."

"But you didn't say the words so how could you be?"

"Olaf was not your father," Emilie explained almost in a whisper.

Marcus was at first stunned. King Eric was his father and his mother's lawful husband? How could the King have dishonoured his mother in this manner?

Marcus always believed that Olaf was his father, and yet he looked nothing like the man or the man who he thought was his half-brother. When he was young he had imagined a different father.

Did any of this really matter? King Eric hadn't acknowledged his kinship to Marcus. He had been denied yet again by another father. What made him so unworthy of their affections and guidance? Was it the very thing that made him Marcus his gifts that made him so different then everyone else? Mother had always told him that those were his strengths, not weaknesses. She had pointed out differences in nature, even showing him snowflakes. She had always been his buffer against the cruelty of the world. She had explained that no two snowflakes were alike, so why shouldn't people be so? This hurt but he would transition on, the pain would halt, he always refocused on what was important.

His mother and her comfort were important. Ingrid he loved, so she too was his priority but could he trust Ingrid? She acted oddly leaving them in a locked room. Ingrid had defended them from Haken, but Haken had said he was betrothed to her so how could he continue to think she might be his?

Marcus found the need to calm himself counting and began to tally the bricks on the fireplace. Marcus suddenly stopped totalling the slabs. How odd, why was there a fireplace? If this was a storage room as Ingrid had told him, she'd lied to Marcus. What more had she told untruths about?

Marcus was upset Emilie could tell. He was calculating the bricks on the fireplace in the storage room.

"Do you hate me Marcus? You are not saying a word to me."

"Mother, never doubt my love for you. We have unity that cannot be broken. You have protected me loved me and sacrificed for me. I will love you even if the King never acknowledges either of us. I shall give him his foul books explain how Ragnor has deceived him and be done with him. We shall go back to our village ad live."

"What of Ingrid?" Emilie asked.

"We shall see mother. She has lied to me and we must find a way to get out of her as I fear she may betray us."

"But how will we do that? We're locked in this room."

"Ah but I have a found a way mother. There's a latch her on the fireplace and if I'm right a passageway will lie behind this wall."

Marcus then triggered the lever. As Marcus predicted, a wall opened and they stepped into a passageway. Emilie grabbed the lit candles from the storage wall and handed one to Marcus. They entered the passageway, closing the door behind them. Emilie was terrified, it was dark dusty and there were cobwebs everywhere. Emilie feared that some of them were probably not cobwebs, but spider webs that were now settling in her hair. She brushed the webs out of her hair, hoping she was wrong.

"Mother, I think this handle might open into a room shall I move it?" Marcus asked.

"Yes but be cautious. There maybe someone in the room and we must not be caught."

Marcus slowly opened the door and peered through the slit. Looking into the darkened room, Marcus saw no one. Scrutinising the room he saw a huge canopy bed and a wardrobe up against the wall, next to it. On the wall were two swords one overlapping the other.

Marcus pulled Emilie out of the passageway and into the room. He then went to a door and peered out into a hallway. "Mother it is a bedroom. It is night, no one occupies it. We are safe, you can rest here. In the morning we will find the King and all will be finished then we can go home."
"But where will you sleep, my son?" Emilie asked looking around the room.
"I will sleep on the floor if you will spare one of those blankets and a pillow."

Marcus was soon asleep but Emilie found herself still awake. She had noticed another door hidden. It was not the one Marcus had found to the hall. She pried opened the door to see another bedroom. She glanced over at the canopy king size bed, to hear a rhythmic breathing coming from the bed.

She tip-toed slowly over to the bed and covered her mouth, gasping, for in the bed was King Eric. Should she wake him now, or wait until morning?

Emilie gasped as King Eric's eyes opened.

"Emilie? If this is a dream I don't want to wake up. How I have longed for you all these years." King Eric cried pulling her into the bed with him.
"You don't even love me. You threw me away like the bath water," protested Emilie.

"I love you more than life itself. I had to protect you there were many people who wanted to kill me. They wouldn't have hesitated to kidnap, or kill you. I protected you and you used it to betray me, marrying another." Eric exclaimed hurt.

"You left without even a word. You abandoned me penniless and with child. I was pregnant with your son. My father forced me to marry Olaf. I thought you would come and save me at the last moment but you didn't. I didn't even say the words yet the priest said we were married. How am I supposed to feel about your *'I love yo*u' declaration?" Emilie complained.

"You could believe me but your story makes no sense, what happened to the money I left for you?"

"What money?" Emilie demanded.

"I left the money with your father. It is obvious we were both betrayed. A tangle of lies one after another to keep us apart." King Eric explained.

"All these years...,"began Emilie crying.

"All these years and we both still love each other." King Eric explained, "I love you Emilie. There has never been anyone else for me. We will tell the kingdom you are still my Queen."

"I love you too but won't this cause problems for you? You can't sacrifice everything for me." cried Emilie, through weeping.

"It isn't a sacrifice. Without you there are is only shade, no sunshine. So being without you is more of a problem."

Eric then wiped away her tears and began kissing her passionately.

"Eric. Marcus is in the other room," Emilie protested.

"Then we'll need to be quiet," King Eric replied laughing and removing her garments as she joined in to help him.

A short while later satiated, Emilie put on her shift and promptly fell asleep by an already asleep Eric. They were both awoken by the bedroom door to the hallway opening and two men coming in with swords drawn.

Emilie screamed.

Marcus heard the scream, recognized it as his mother's and grabbed the two swords from the wall, before entering the room from which he heard the scream.

Seeing King Eric in bed with his mother the two of them naked gave him a start. However realizing the two men were advancing on his mother and father, he threw a sword to King Eric and took a stance to fight the men. His father joined him. Clashes of swords rang out, the fighting fast and furious. Marcus was glad of all those times he had fight with a wooden sword, to beat off bullies. This sword was heavier, but he was holding his own and had even laid blows down on his opponent.

Marcus had a few nicks but nothing serious. He managed to wound his adversary with a blow to the fleshy part of the shoulder. The man dropped his sword, though he was also bleeding from the stomach. King Eric had also managed to wound his foe striking a blow to the man's heart. The man lay dying on the floor.

"Marcus take your mother and hide next door. I must find out who is behind this before I announce that your mother is my wife and you are my son," King Eric ordered.
"Ragnor took your money. He's probably behind this attack as well," Marcus announced.
"You may be correct my son. I have to take steps to make sure we are all safe. The kingdom must also be protected for one day you will be the wise leader who leads it."

"Thank you Father, but these men could still be a danger to you. We should tie them up."

"We have no rope," protested King Eric.

"We will use the tassels from the bed curtains," Marcus declared.

After the men were tied hand and foot, Marcus relieved obeyed the king taking his mother to hide next door. King Eric then summoned the guards.

~0~

King Eric opened the door to his guards and found himself at sword point. The guards were closely followed by Haken and Ragnor.

"You oaf did you think I'd continue to allow you to be King? You are a disgrace," Ragnor stated then laughed, "Haken tells me that the boy I thought was my kin is your spawn. Where is he? He's not in the room Haken saw him in."

"Boy, what boy? I have not seen the boy, since I left him working on my books. What are you talking about Ragnor? Emilie was married to your brother. He is your nephew. Do you deny him as your brother Olaf did?" King Eric asked.

"Do not think you can fool me with your gabble. I know now that Marcus is your son and Emilie the unfaithful whore is your spouse," Ragnor shouted, piercing King Eric's arm slightly with the sword.

"Do you really feel the need to cut me this way? I have treated you like family." King Eric pleaded.

"Are you delusional old man? You treated me like you did everyone, as chess pieces for your amusement, servants to you for your every whim. What about your people?"

"Ragnor I love and honour my subjects every day, looking after their wellbeing. You have been deceived by this little worm Haken. He sought my ward's hand in marriage and I refused it; so he goes around making up lies to hurt me. I do not know where they are. They have disappeared from the castle."

Marcus heard all of this through the closed door, anger building up inside him, both for Ragnor and King Eric. They had both denied him yet again. How could Marcus trust either of them?

"Haken have you lied to me?" threatened Ragnor turning his sword on Haken and placing it at his neck.

"I swear I have not my Lord."

"Where are they Eric?" Ragnor asked menacingly.

"You will address me as your lawful King, ordained by God," King Eric demanded.

"You call yourself King? You are a joke in the kingdom. You are a buffoon who sits on the throne and knows nothing of what goes on in his kingdom. Bah you probably don't know where they are. You didn't even know it was I, who took from your coffers."

"I know that you are a treasonous pig who endangers the good of the kingdom and its people. You will pay for this treachery, Ragnor," King Eric replied.

"You and whose army? I control the guards now a little greasing of the palms and allegiances change," Ragnor exclaimed laughing.

"Do your worst, Ragnor but you better hope you haven't underestimated your favour, miscalculation could be hazardous to your health," King Eric answered.

"First I will give you time to fear your demise. In three days hence you shall be publicly beheaded and I will be crowned King. Your cousin has said so. After I find your spawn your line will end."

"Marcus is not my son, though I wish he was. I can't believe you trusted my cousin! You are a fool Ragnor. My cousin wants to be King. His birth status denies his ambition, so he seeks to rid the kingdom of me and take my throne. Once he is, you will meet your demise. I will be in Valhalla, will you?"

Marcus realized with shame his father was trying to save him. Marcus went to rush through the door and save his father but his mother pulled him back.

"There are too many Marcus. We will save your father, but first we must be away. They must not find us or we cannot help. Come we must hide in the tunnels until we can find Ingrid and find help to overturn Ragnor and his men," Emilie whispered.

Marcus and Emilie then quietly scurried into the tunnels to hide and find help.

~0~

T he tunnel was dark and seemed to go on forever.

Where did it come out Marcus could seem to find a door that opened. Marcus was worried what would they do if his father wasn't saved? Ragnor wanted the both of them dead. They would have to flee the country if he couldn't be stopped.

"Mother who can we ask for help?"
"We should find Ingrid. She is an intelligent woman, she may know men we can summon who are nearby," Emilie answered.
"But we don't even know where Father was taken," Marcus insisted, not even realizing he called King Eric father.
"Your father asked them where they were taking him. Did you not hear?"
"Tell me what you heard."
"Your father got Ragnor to tell him they were taking him to the hunting lodge where they took us. So see we do know where he is."
"But how can we find Ingrid?"
"My son you keep throwing up barriers. Think positively. Remember when you were young and you'd falter I'd teach you how to overcome those feelings."
"Yes, I must think positively and all will be overcome. One, two three...Marcus began but he stopped as he thought he heard something in the tunnel.

Marcus tilted his head to listen again.

"Mother I hear someone in the tunnels hide behind me up against the wall. We must not let them find us."
"Marcus?" a voice carried through the tunnel.
"Ingrid?" asked Marcus surprised recognizing her voice.

"Oh thank goodness, I found you Marcus. Some of these tunnels go on forever. You should have stayed in the storeroom."

"Why so your fiancé Haken could turn us in to Ragnor?" Marcus asked.

"He is not my fiancé, I would never marry him. I don't love him," Ingrid exclaimed with great emotion.

"Who do you love?" Marcus asked softly.

"I love you," Ingrid blurted without meaning to, than he heard her cover her mouth.

"You love me? I love you. Marry me!" Marcus exclaimed touching her arm.

"Are you sure you barely know me," Ingrid answered.

"I am sure I love you and want you to be my wife."

"Then yes, I will marry you," exclaimed Ingrid leaping into his arms as Emilie moved out of the way.

"Oh sorry, we forgot you were there Madame Emilie," Ingrid apologized, noticing Emilie for the first time.

"I gathered that. You will be my daughter soon; but that also involves great risk. King Eric has been seized by Ragnor. He believes Eric's cousin is helping him to take the throne," Emilie explained.

"Fool, doesn't he realize that Eric's cousin wants to reign himself? You called him Eric? I knew my research was correct. You were his wife."

"No, I am his legal wife," Emilie admitted.

Ingrid's steps faltered and she seem to shrink before Marcus' eyes, even in the inky blackness.

"Oh, no you look like him Marcus, that's what I kept seeing in you. I'll never be allowed to marry the King's son and heir," Ingrid cried.

"My father will not decide my marriage. He married for love and so shall I," Marcus reassured her.

"I am foolish to think of myself and my future when the kingdom stands in jeopardy," Ingrid commented.

"How can we raise men to help my husband? Ragnor has said he will publically execute him in three days," Emilie asked.

"I know of some men loyal to the King, but I have hope that the King of Norway and his men will arrive in time."

"It has not been announced that he would visit, why would the King of Norway, Eric's cousin suddenly arrive?" asked Emilie.

"When I found you prisoner at the hunting lodge I sent for him. He is in Bjorko. He is nearby in I admit I used the King's seal without permission."

"If he is in Bjorko and he left right away he could arrive anytime now," Marcus concluded.

"In the meantime we need to raise men to fight Ragnor and keep Eric safe. I do not trust Ragnor to keep him alive."

"He'll keep him alive my Queen, but he may torture him."

"Torture? Oh Marcus we must quickly save your father," Emilie exclaimed.

"I know where the key is to King Eric's safe we will need many krona to finance the battle," Ingrid offered.

"It is too dangerous, let me do this," Marcus demanded.

"Marcus, I am the only person that can do this. Ragnor thinks of me as a girl child, stupid and incapable of deceit. He will never believe that I have looted the safe to save the King!" Ingrid explained, "When I have the money I will come to you and all three of us will then approach the men and save the King. Do you trust me to do this?"

"I trust you with my life and my parents. You must go," Marcus replied softly.

"Only when I know you and your Mother are safe will I leave. Go to the end of this corridor and turn right. There is a lever on the wall there Turn it clockwise and you will come out in my bedroom. Wait there for me if you hear anyone coming hiding in my wardrobe."

"I don't like this Ingrid but I will do as you ask the cobwebs in this corridor are making me itch," Marcus complained.

"Remember that I love you Marcus and I will be back soon to make you live up to your promise," Ingrid said kissing Marcus passionately on the lips before he went down the corridor.

Ingrid watched as they proceeded. When Marcus opened the lever, she waved goodbye and then turned the other way in the corridor rapidly disappearing from Marcus view.

Marcus stepped into the room looking both ways to make sure no one was there and then pulled his mother in. Seeing a bowl and some towels they both washed their faces and hands.

Marcus was hungry and so was Emilie but they knew they needed to stay here. Emilie spotted a bowl of fruit and offered Marcus some before taking some herself. They satisfied some of their hunger and waited patiently for Ingrid to return. It seemed like hours before they heard a click in the wall and hid themselves in the wardrobe, in case it was someone other than Ingrid who entered through the tunnel. A few seconds later they heard..."Marcus and Queen Emilie?"

Then the wardrobe opened to Ingrid's smiling face. "Come on you slug we have some men to buy to fight Ragnor," Ingrid exclaimed laughing.

Marcus kissed her and then taking his mother's hand they went back into the tunnel to follow Ingrid who would take them out into the forest where they would find the men.

~0~

I n the forest they travelled quickly looking for Ingrid's suggestions of men to fight for the King. When they came into the nearest village, Marcus called the people together to speak to them.

"I am of the Nilsson family. My name is Magnus Marcus and my father Nicholas Eric is your King. He has been taken prisoner by Ragnor Canute Emune, who seeks my father's throne for his own. Will you fight for your King who has provided for you, given you food in lean years and kept you safe from warring factions, or will you allow the usurper to succeed?"

"We've never heard of you," one man complained.

"I heard tell he was Olaf Emune's son and he was disowned and he became a Magnusson; so he is lying," one man shouted.

"Olaf Emune took me from my lawful husband. The King and he claimed at first that Magnus Marcus was his own, but look at my son, he bares the look of his father."

"He does have the look of the King," agreed another.

"Once more I have proof that I am King Eric's legal wife, which makes me Queen Margaret Marie Emilie. I am your lawful monarch in King Eric's stead. You may call me Queen Emilie," demanded Emilie.

But still there were whispers and no acceptance of Emilie as Queen.

"Who among you can read?" Emilie asked pulling a folded paper out of her bag.

"I can," claimed the man stepping up.

Emilie held fast to the paper but allowed him to read it and the man bent to his knees and exclaimed, "She is our lawful Queen, Long live Queen Emilie."

A cheer rang up from all the villagers and they stepped forward to obey their queen, some of them fell to their knees and shouted, "Long live, Queen Emilie."
"I need your help. We must plan a coup against Ragnor and save our King," Emilie exclaimed.

"My name is Andenon, my father is Ander the King's manservant. I have met the King he would want us to keep you safe my Queen. Let us plan the battle,"Andenon insisted.
"This is my husband I would see him safe. I will go," Emilie demanded.
"Mother you are tired you have not slept well and you need food and rest. We will rescue my father and then he will lead the charge with you by his side, to rid of us of the rabble rouser Ragnor," Marcus asserted.
"Please stay with me Queen Emilie, I am so weary and I could use the company," Ingrid pleaded.
"You need me Ingrid?" Emilie asked.
"I do need your council, will you stay and let Marcus and the men rescue the King and bring him back to us?"
"Very well if you all insist, I will wait, with you, but please men bring my husband and son safely back to me," Emilie conceded.

~0~

Emilie, Ingrid and the other women of the village
waited for Marcus and the other male villagers to come
back. Emilie slept as did Ingrid for a few hours and then
they ate. As dark fell Emilie and Ingrid could wait no more.
Ingrid and Emilie went back to the palace to find what
weapons they could and brought them back to the village.

While Ingrid and Emilie were at the palace, the
blacksmith's wife Birgitta worked diligently making
breastplate armour for all the women she could. Ingrid's
and Emilie's were made first and carefully painted gold.
The blacksmiths wife also managed to find some horses for
some of the women and swords.

At dawn the women banded together. Ingrid and Emilie
dressed in the armour and mounted the horses. Ingrid and
Emilie placed a bow on their left shoulder and a cache of
arrows on their right. A sword was hung in a sheaf on their
left hips. The other women also mounted what horses and
even donkeys they could find and donned their gear. Some
women who could find no mounts walked swiftly behind
the merry band.

Every woman over the age of sixteen joined them except
those expecting who stayed to care for the children with the
younger women.

As they neared the hunting lodge the women gave out a
fearful cry to scare their foe. A man in the hunting lodge
peered out saw the gleaming armour in the early morning
light and screamed. Another man looked out.

"It's the ride of the Valkyries," cried Esjoborn who Ingrid
recognized as one of her cousins.
"Let me see Esjoborn. You know you are given to fancy,"
demanded Gunnar.

Gunnar looked out and gasped then he yelled "I'm not ready for Valhalla. What would save me?"

"They think we are the Valkyrie!" Ingrid whispered to Emilie, "Let him continue to think so."

"Give up the King and his son and you will not die," demanded Emilie in a fierce cold voice, pretending to be the queen of the Valkyrie.

"If I give up the King and his son, Ragnor will kill me when he comes."

"I will guarantee your safety should you and your men swear allegiance to King Nicholas Eric but hear me now should you refuse you shall not see Valhalla but die in battle here and now," Emilie offered.

The door to the hunting lodge closed and Emilie thought she had lost them. They would have to charge in and save Eric and Marcus she decided. Seconds later the door opened King Eric marched out unbound followed by Marcus. The men from the village then paraded behind them. Esjoborn and Gunnar followed with their soldiers, their arms all raised in the air.

"Emilie? Ingrid? My dears you saved us," King Eric cried kissing Emilie on the lips and then Ingrid on the cheek. Marcus kissed Ingrid and said, "I always knew I was in the presence of a Valkyrie."

"We should put these men to death, as they would have us," King Eric exclaimed, narrowing his eyes and looking angry.

"These men have promised their fealty to you my king. We will not harm them. I have given my word and yours. I know ask them to kneel before us three and swear allegiance to the family Nilsson and their King Nicholas Eric," Emilie demanded.

Esjoborn and Gunnar quickly knelt before the king and his family followed by their men. All swore allegiance and total loyalty to the King and his family.

"Come must be away and hide in the woods. Ragnor is coming later this morning to check on his prisoners. We must catch him unaware and surround him," King Eric insisted.

They crept into the woods to wait, alert any sound. Hours went by and they heard the sound of swiftly approaching horses. King Eric and Marcus and all took their places ready to surround Ragnor and take him alive. They didn't have long to wait before the thunder of horses was heard.

Ragnor strode through the forest on a great white stead his sword at his side. He tried to look regal but missed since he didn't sit up straight in the saddle. King Eric and his men surrounded Ragnor's men easily and subdued them, before Ragnor even realized they were no longer beside, or behind him. King Eric then approached Ragnor knocking him from his horse. Ragnor quickly regained his feet and swung his sword slashing King Eric's arm. King Eric's men quickly moved as if to subdue Ragnor; but King Eric waved them away. King Eric clanged his sword against Ragnor's who met him blow for blow. The clash of the pugilists went on for what seemed a half an hour to Marcus, still with no clear winner though each bore the scars and blood from the battle. Finally the skirmish was ended when King Eric's sword hit a target which made Ragnor fall down to the ground. King Eric stared into at Ragnor's face. Ragnor looked drawn and near death's door. It became obvious Ragnor's heart was bleeding out fast, as he threw down his weapon in concession.

"My brother knew he was your son and kept Marcus from you. Emilie was too good for either of you. She should have been my queen. You weren't fit to be King you with your game leg and your broken son, that child of the cuckoo's nest," Ragnor growled through broken breath.

"I pity you. You were given opportunity money and privilege only to squander it. Hate and envy ate you up so that you couldn't see even a man who has a crippled leg can defend his country and take care of its people and a that a child who is nurtured and loved can become a man his people can revere and love," Eric stated.

"He is still addled."

"Marcus has a brilliant mind that the likes of you could never understand. He will lead his people and his country into prosperity with his intellect.

"I would tell you something that you alone should hear," Ragnor began, motioning at King Eric to come closer. Marcus felt uneasy about this and told his father, "Don't trust him he could stab you up close."

"The boy is correct, if I had a weapon I would kill you and leave you on this battle field while I would go to Valhalla. But what I wanted to tell you is that I really am the boy's Uncle. You have killed your brother," Ragnor exclaimed in ragged breaths .then drew his last breath and died.

King Eric appeared to crumble and Emilie knew this was had to be Ragnor's last trick to harm King Eric.

"It was lie my love. He had the look of his father about him. You met Ragnor's father, do you not see it?" Emilie asked.

"What would I do without you my love?" King Eric asked realizing the truth in Emilie's words.

"You'll never have to find out," Emilie claimed slipping her arm in his.

Marcus looked on this amazed and pleased at how much his father loved his mother. His mother would be loved, cosseted but allowed to be Emilie. She would be happy he didn't have to feel guilty that he was leaving her home to be with Ingrid.

A cheer rang up from King Eric's men "Long Live the King long live King Eric. Long Live the Queen, our own Queen Emilie and long live our beloved Prince Magnus Marcus."

King Eric took up residence again in Drottingholm Palace with Emilie by his side. Some in the Kingdom who had always been convinced that Marcus was the cuckoo in Olaf Emune's nest wondered if he was truly the King's heir, others were convinced they only had to look at the young man to see his father's look about him.

Others from Marcus' village, where he grew up, tried to tell others they thought him strange and peculiar. These people's opinions were quickly silenced by the people who had met Marcus in the weeks, since he came to the palace. They pointed out how Marcus had risked his all and demanded their loyalty and allegiance to the King. They asked these villagers if they would fight for their King, the way the young prince had? The villagers from Marcus village quickly agreed, lest their loyalty be brought into question. They began to see the young man in a new light a hero in the realm.

All the people of the kingdom then became excited that not only did their King now had a wife, but also an heir. King Eric had decreed a royal wedding would take place in two weeks' time between Prince Magnus Marcus and Lady Ingrid Jägerhon, Countess of Riksgränsen, the King's ward and preparations in earnest had begun.

The people would celebrate the nuptials with a grand party and plenty of wine and food. A party would bring all the people together under his majesty.

The day arrived, the sun shone bright as the bride in her splendour was brought down the aisle to her groom. Marcus grinned as Ingrid beamed back. The priest married the couple and then gave blessings for a happy fruitful marriage for the couple. He also renewed the King and Queen's vows.

Emilie smiled at her son and her new daughter, her hand in Eric's and marvelled at how life had changed for her since Marcus was born. Olaf had been convinced the boy was switched and maybe to Olaf he was. After all he wasn't Olaf's son, but she wouldn't have her son any other way. He was different some might say but that is what made Marcus the son she adored.

She looked forward to the day now that Marcus and Ingrid would come to her and tell her she would be a grandmother; but until then she and King Eric would try to get back some of the time they had lost. And maybe, just maybe, she might have a surprise for them all; as she might bear another heir for King Eric in about eight months, if all went well. She laughed at the fact that she had believed Marcus to be of the cuckoo's nest. Marcus was a son that would make any parent proud. She would welcome another child from the cuckoo's nest or any other child they might have.

"Life was good in their kingdom." Emilie thought, "May god bring light and love and may the kingdom continue to be happy."

~0~

Bear Brave

My hair brushed to a fine silk, hung down my back in ringlets, which refused to leave. The attendant placed the finest white veil over my face and head, hiding me from view. The veil luminous, as gold flecks were embroidered throughout it, yet so thick I couldn't see through it. I wondered again why I had to finish this and then I remembered...people depended on me.

Scared, I kept telling myself just get through this. As I marched down the long hall and into the inner sanctum of the beast, I heard the attendant leave and the doors slam closed. I was living a story out of the Brothers Grimm how was this possible? I peeked through a small hole in the veil and saw a huge dark room. I counted at least twenty dark black curtains covering what I assumed were windows around the room. Had someone died? It looked like a house in mourning. I grew more afraid would I even be welcomed?

I fumbled around finding first floor to ceiling treasures of gold and jewels in containers then two chairs covered in gold and satin brocade. I sat down being careful to arrange my gold silk dress carefully around me to present the best picture.

I glanced around the room again and comprehended it wasn't totally dark; lamps flickered on low, in the corners of the room. I breathed a sigh of relief when I realized I was alone, I could still flee I thought and then I remembered what would happen if I did. I would finish what I had started.

I sat there for hours wondering if I would die from hunger or thirst first; when the door to the room opened with a thud. I wanted to scream and run but my duty must be done. I straightened up and stood up from the chair to await the beast. The beast from what I could see through the tiny hole in the veil and the darkness of the room, stood as a tall as a giant. Too dark for me to see his face I still saw that he was over seven feet tall. In shadow I saw his arms swing as he walked across the room. He startled when he saw me standing there.

I was more stunned fairy-tales were real? I was sure they were joking when they sent me here. That they had just found an unusual husband for me but after all I was the youngest daughter. Who cared about a spare anyway?

"What have we here? Have the villagers brought me yet another of what they think is treasure?" he asked, as he reached out to touch me.

The beast unwrapped me like a present, removing my veil. He touched my hair and I grew frightened, other sacrifices had come back with tales of the beast screaming at them and then wrapping them up in rugs to be returned to the villagers. I could not be returned, if I were then all would be lost. The village owed a great debt to the beast and they had decided I could be the only payment. I would do my duty.

"So they've sent me another woman. When will they stop? I didn't want the marauders near the village anymore and then they did. The village was lucky they came at night, for I do not go out during the day.

 I tried to look over my shoulder and into his eyes, but I could not see them in the darkness.

"Don't you have a tongue, or have they cut it out?"
"I am sorry, my lord. I did not know you wished me to speak," I answered meekly.
"Politeness? And so it begins another simpering miss, who begs me not to ravish her," he laughed.

I smiled to put him at ease, though I shook in my boots.

"Go," he commanded.

I could not go back in disgrace they would think me dishonoured anyway I must remain and do the job they didn't truly expect me to do.

"Please sir, let me stay. I can make your home more habitable," I offered.
"You've seen only my treasure room, why would you think my home uncivilized?"
"I beg your pardon sir, I did not say that. I only offered to..."
"You offered to clean, like a scullery maid. I can clean myself. You are a great lady, are you not?"
"I am a lady, and a princess," I admitted.
"And you think me a beast?"
"Oh no, sir, I do not," I lied.
"You lie prettily enough. Are you clever? Can you play the harpsichord?"
"I can and I can sing as well. I am told I have the voice of an angel."
"There in the corner is a harpsichord and a sheet of music. Regale me with your talent."

"I fear I cannot see the music, or the keys, my lord."
"Cover your head with this veil again, whilst I light the
lamp in the corner. You must not look at me, only look at
the harpsichord. If you look at me, I will have to kill you is
that understood?"
"Yes," I answered.

He walked me to the harpsichord and bade me sit. I did so
and then after he lit the lamp, he removed my veil and told
me to perform. The song near the harpsichord was a
favourite of mine, *'Drink to Me Only with Thine Eyes'*.

As my voice rose in joy and I gave myself over to the
music, the room was transformed, roses bloomed in the
room and light filled the room surrounding me. I felt
exhilarated and like love surrounded me. Somehow, I knew
all this came from him whom they called the beast, but was
he a beast? I wanted to look back at him, but I grew afraid
of his threat to slay me.

"Your voice is golden and has brought me joy. Put the veil
on and come with me," the beast bade me when I finished.

He took me to a bedroom and I grew afraid again but then
he slammed the door and I heard a bolt thrown on the other
side. Through the door I heard "Eat the food I placed at
your bedside and sleep well my lady. I will return after you
rest."

I looked around in the centre of the room was a huge four
poster bed with pure cotton white voile bed curtains and
white satin sheets with a white cotton bedspread. Beside the
bed on a small table as the beast had promised was food and
drink. Maybe he was not a beast? I reasoned, had he not
gave me food drink and a place to sleep?

I ate and drank greedily and found my eyes quickly closing. There had been drugs in the food or drink I reasoned, but who had prepared it I was my last thought, before I surrendered to sleep.

I awoke to night and a chairwoman who entered my room.

"Surprised you're still here, I am. Have you seen himself?" the chairwoman asked, "He's not a true Beast but ...."
"Then you've seen him?"
"The beast? No, if I did I wouldn't work here, now would I?"
"Then how do you get your orders?" I asked.
"He leaves me notes. You look familiar, do I know you?"
"I am Princess Cecilia, of the kingdom of Umbra."
"Princess? Forgive me Princess Cecilia for speaking so familiar. You are my sovereign, princess. I met your mother once. She was the better of all your father's brides."
"You met my mother?"
"I did, many years ago, she visited my village. Queen Celeste was kind to me, protecting me from a tyrannical lord."
"But Queen Celeste is not my mother. My mother is the present queen."
"You are the spitting image of Queen Celeste. She got me a new job and gave me coinage. I can't believe that you are not hers. So I'll be kind to you and tell you leave now. Don't stay with the Beast. Something could happen to you."
"I cannot leave. My kingdom owes a great debt to the Beast. I have been sent as payment. May I know your name?" I queried.
"My name is Anna Fellows mistress. But I must say even if it should anger you, the kingdom does you a grave injustice. I thought you had a sister, why wasn't she sent to the Beast?"
"My sister is frail in body and soul and could not meet the Beast. She would shriek and faint. The beast would hate that."
"Who volunteered to send you here?"

"My mother and my sister; but they only wanted to save the kingdom."

"Oh dearie, they have done you wrong. The kingdom is safe. The Beast likes to be left alone. All they did was to get rid of the competition. With no sons now…"

"What has happened to my brothers?"

"They've succumbed to an illness. Some whisper it is poison that killed them. With you gone too, who will take the throne but sister? They should give you the badge of stupidity," Anna exclaimed, then remembering my title, she blanched and said, "Forgive me I forgot myself princess."

"You are forgiven but also sadly mistaken," I uttered.

"I risk your ire princess, but alas they have conspired to rid themselves of the very person who could protect the King."

"No, they wouldn't they love me and my father."

"Do they now? Why didn't your father the King speak up?"

"Father has been ill."

"Has he now? You are a liability to their plans. Do you know that he is safe with them? Maybe they are the reason he's ill."

"No, if what you insist is true, he is not safe. But I cannot leave. I and my kingdom owe the Beast. He has not told me to leave yet and I cannot leave until he bids me do so. He found pleasure in my music last night. If I give him some of my time and music, we will fulfil our debt and I will be able to go home."

"I could go and watch over him, but then the Beast would not have his housekeeping done," the chairwoman offered.

"I could do the housekeeping. If you'd watch over my father until I can leave. I'll gladly pay you once I come home to the palace," I insisted.

"You, my princess? You've probably never cooked or cleaned in your lifetime. How would you manage?"

"Could you show me before you go to my father?" I asked boldly.

"I guess I could. If you are able to learn then I will go to him," the chairwoman promised.

"Thank you Anna."

So that is how I learned to cook and clean. The Beast never appeared in the daylight so I easily hid the cleaning and cooking from him. In the evenings he would appear after dark, the rooms in full blackness. Two weeks had passed and still he didn't know. I had heard nothing from Anna but I hoped she would send a message soon.

That night taking my arm he led me from my room and into the dark drawing room where he would have me sing and play for my supper. Each time I sang beautiful flowers appeared like magic. I decided the Beast was quick with his hands and pulled them out of the darkness to enchant me. The beauty of the flowers always surprised me with first roses, then daisies, then lilies, the scents filling my noise and my voice with joy. But still the Beast would not let me see him in the light. I grew curious to why he was always in shadow. Was he truly beast like? Did he have the head of a lion or the limbs of a horse? Why did he hid from me?

"I can't keep calling you princess. Don't you think you could tell me your name?"
"If you tell me your name," I requested boldly.
"Very well, my name is Barrett. People who are familiar with me call me Barry."
"You name means Bear Brave. Are you a bear, Barrett?"

Barrett laughed a belly laugh of denial and then demanded, "And your name princess?"
"Cecilia," I answered.
"Aw, that explains it, you are the blind sight one," Barrett exclaimed.
"No, my name means musical or gifted one."
"That suits you as well Cecilia."
"Thank you Barrett."
"Now that we've been introduced, did you stroll through the gardens today?" he asked abruptly.
"Why do you ask that?"

"I smell lemon on your clothes."

I had polished the copper pots with lemon like Anna had showed me. Did he suspect?

"I picked a lemon and made some lemonade," I answered.
"May I have some? I love lemonade," the beast answered.
"There isn't any I lied," I admitted.
"Where did Anna go, and why have you been cooking and cleaning? I pay her to keep the castle clean," the beast asked.

I was frightened, was he angry? He had seemed so friendly, but I heard the stories from the other women; would he turn on me the way the other women said he had on them?

"Do not look at me that way. I have not mistreated you. Just tell me where is Anna, princess."
"She went to check on my father."
"Why?"
"He's been ill. She had suspicions that he may have been poisoned."
"Poisoned but who would do such a thing?"
"I think she's wrong but..."
"But you couldn't take a chance because you love your father."
"You understand? I could go myself..."
"No it's better that Anna went I enjoy your company Cecilia."

So I find myself enjoying the company of Barry and still I haven't heard from Anna. I fear that my trust in her wanes.

~0~

T he day after this conversation I awoke to knocking at my bedroom door. Opening the door I found a young woman. She told me Barry had hired her and her young man, to care for the castle. Agnes was a talkative sort, and soon told me her whole story. Her name was Agnes and her husband's name was Albert. They were very young, only fifteen years old. Agnes told me she was pregnant. Barry had found a priest to marry them and offered them jobs. Anna explained that even though now her child would be legitimate, her parents would not speak to her. I must have shown pity for Anna went on to exclaim that she had a job, a good husband, and a baby on the way. She was blessed. Even if Anna came back she would still have a job. Barry hid a heart of gold behind his Beast persona and I found myself falling in love with him.

Days went by and I enjoy my evenings with Barry. We waltzed to his music box and I have felt free and safe in his arms, despite the extreme darkness he insisted upon. Barry surprised me with little gifts, like that music box and flowers.

I'd love to see him...really see his face, but he stays in the shadows. Does he feel that I would gasp at or reject his appearance? I do not think I am that shallow obviously others have rejected him and called him Beast. No wonder he doesn't trust me. These people had been so damaging to him, but I will make him feel special. I will make him trust me. He cares for me I know he does.

"I'd like to go to the shops tomorrow and get some ribbon. May I, Barry?"
"No."

I must have done something to indicate my displeasure for he started explaining his reasons.

"There are dark forces that could harm you there. I would feel better if you sent Agnes and Albert," Barry answered me.

I tried to answer but I knew I would sound like I whined so I kept silent.
"Please, Cecilia, for me?" Barry begged, "I could bear if anything happened to you."
"For you," I conceded.

The next day I waited anxiously for Agnes and Albert to come back. I sent Agnes with a note so she could pick up some fabric to make Barry a present. I planned to make Barry a fine red shirt out of silk he could wear. Agnes came back with the material and the other things I asked for. I sensed Agnes wanted to say something to me but she said nothing.

I gave thanks for my love of embroidery. I had been laughed at and told it an act unfitting of a princess, but it prepared me to make the shirt. I had used my arms to measure him when we danced and used those same measurements to make the shirt. I went to the sewing room in the castle and set about the afternoon stitching the shirt. Some hours later as the sun began to set my fingers were cramped and bore many jabs from the needle but the shirt was finished. I inspected my work and the embroidery I had also put on the collar and down each side of the front. I felt pleased with myself.

"Miss, the Beast has called supper is laid out in the great room. You best hurry before it is cold," Agnes told me coming into the room.

Then she saw the shirt in my hands and her mouth went wide.

"Why miss, I would never have believed a great lady like you could create such artistry with the needle."
"Do you think he'll like it?" I asked.
"Miss any man would be pleased to wear such a fine garment made with loving hands."
"Am I that obvious?" I asked.
"Miss every time you speak of the master, your face lights up and you glow."
"I'd better hurry. But what can I wrap the shirt in?"
"I have an old fabric flour sack I washed. It would become a dress after I dyed it."
"You'd give this to me?"
"Of course, Princess."
"Thank-you, Agnes."

A few minutes later Agnes came back with the flour bag, she had clearly washed and handed it to me.

"If you give me this flour bag then you have to let me give you some material to make your dress. Here take this cloth," I offered, after I put the shirt inside the bag.
"But Princess Cecilia wasn't this for your own dress?"
"Yes, but I have many bolts of material that you and Albert procured. Take this one, it is a brilliant blue and would complement your lovely red hair and blue eyes."
"I would love to but it would be right. Would it?" Agnes asked fingering the cloth lovingly.
"It would be perfectly alright besides it's a gift. Now you would want to anger me by not accepting my gift would you? And call me miss I much prefer it to princess," I countered.
"No, princess, I mean miss. Thank you for this lovely material. I'll make a lovely dress after the baby is born."
"Why not make it now? After the baby is born, I shall send you to buy a bolt of material that you can then surprise your Albert with," I offered.

"Thank you again, miss. I heard something in the village perhaps you should know," Agnes offered tentatively.

"What was that? Does someone conspire against Barry?"

"No, miss. I heard the King was on his deathbed."

"What? Are you sure you heard this?"

"I'm afraid so. I heard it from more than one in the marketplace."

"I need to go to my father but how?"

"Hurry, miss! Do not tarry longer, it is pastime to sup with the Master," Agnes cautioned.

I hurried into the dark room and felt around as I always did for my utensils and plate. As always the plate had been filled with food. I offered the shirt to him after I finished the food.

"What is this?" he asked, as he took the bundle and opened it.

"A present."

"Cecilia, you made me a shirt? But how?"

"I sewed it all afternoon," I answered.

"This is indeed a fine treasure," Barry answered.

"Barry, Agnes told me of something she heard in the village," I began.

"You sound distressed. If someone has hurt you with their gossip, I will make them sorry," he snarled.

"No, that's not it. Agnes heard my father dies. I must go to him."

"You must not leave me...,"Barry cried sounding like a wounded animal.

"Barry I will return but I must go to my father and see how my sister fares."

"What if she conspires with your mother?"

"I must go. I love my father and my sister."

"Then you must promise yourself to me first and be my wife," Barry declared.

"Marry you?"

"You do not want to marry me?"

"Of course, I do my darling Bear," I answered.

"I will fetch a priest we shall be married tonight after you sign a blood oath to return to me with in a fortnight."

"But I thought you trusted me," I protested.

"I do, but should you break your oath then dire consequences will happen."

"Fine then," I said cutting my hand with my knife and writing a vow with my finger in blood on my napkin, but I understood it was just his ego that needed this vow, it helped him trust me.

Barry bound my hand with his napkin and rushed to my side.

"Cecilia, I am sorry I tested you. I wasn't really going to have you shed your blood. But now that I have your promise we will be married. The morning after our marriage you will take Albert and four of his men to guard you so that you might return to me in a fortnight."

"I promise I will come back to you. I will always come back to you for you are my heart."

"And you are mine. I trust you, I know you will."

So that night we married and I spent an enchanting night with my husband. In the morning I awoke and he was still beside me. Though he had asked me not to look at his face I could not resist and I looked. His hair was red and long to his shoulders. It felt like silk when I touched it. I saw one half of his face; the left side under a red beard had pinkness to it, I recognized as a healed burn. It was also scarred. As I looked his pale blue eyes opened and to my shock, I realized though he looked at me, those clouded eyes did not see me. Barry was blind.

"How could you, Cecilia. How could you betray me this way?" Barry raged.

"I'm sorry," was all I could croak out.

"Now you know you're married to a scarred blind man, not a strong Beast. Wife you still made me a promise to return and if you do not I shall reign vengeance on your kingdom and your family."

"Barry..."

"I would have no lies from you wife. Go from me now wife, but remember my vow."

I spent the rest of the morning preparing for my journey. My heart truly broken, for I had betrayed Barry's trust. He'd never forgive me, but I had no choice I must go to my father. I would try to make him forgive me when I returned. Just when I thought that I would leave with my husband's ire still ringing in my ears, he came to me.

Barry kissed my lips softly, a tender goodbye and then he begged forgiveness, "Forgive me for threatening your family. I would not harm a hair on their head. I hope that one day you may look on this face with love. But know that because my heart goes with you, I beg you come back soon."

My heart went out to my Beast who thought his imperfections would make me not love him.

"I love you Barry," I cried and kissed him. but I do not think he believed it, yet.

I promised I would and I went back to Umbra to be with my father, four riders and a driver with me to protect me.

~0~

Albert drove the carriage as a coachman and the four horsemen rode beside. The moon hid behind clouds, as we entered the village. All the homes were shuttered and dark. We arrived at the castle and were set upon by guards who tried to not let me pass. Albert ran interference and we entered my father's room ahead of them. Albert barred the door outside preventing them from entering.

My sister Sibylline kneeled at the side of my father's bed his left hand in hers. I went to his right side and took his right hand. My father looked ashen and grave. His breath was laboured and I feared all I had heard was true. As I leaned to look at him closer he opened his eyes.

"Celeste is it time?" he sputtered through torturous breath.
"Father it's not mother, it's me, Cecilia," I answered.
"Cecilia, my darling girl, you're safe? The Beast that Helena hoped would kill you, it did not harm you?"
"No, father."
"Thank the heavens. Take your sister to safety...not long now."
"I will father."
"Will you Cecilia?" Helena chuckled as she stepped through a secret door in the wall.
"Please Hel...ena...spare my children," my father begged.
 "She won't harm her own daughter," I reassured my father.

I walked over to my father.

"I have no daughter; you foolish child. You're too late anyway your father is now dead. See for yourself."

I reached for my father and could feel no breath from his lips. She had killed him. I sprung at her, but Sibylline pulled me back. I calmed myself realizing that I had to save Sibylline and myself.

"I don't understand mother. Sibylline and I are your flesh and blood. Would you harm us?"
"Cecilia, Cecilia, amply named. Your mother was Queen Celeste. We pretended she wasn't your mama. Your father thought that would be best for you. Months after her reported death it took her baby.
"What?"
"It was so delicious the only person who was with her I had killed. Your foolish father thought she died in early pregnancy while he was fighting the kingdom of Georgis."
"Then your my step-mother?"
"Listen up Cecilia it gets worse. I put Celeste in the dungeons fed her so the babe within her would live and got your father to marry me, consoling him in his grief. Then I conveniently became 'pregnant' with your sister. When the time came to give 'birth' I went into confinement while your father awaited news of your sister's birth. Lucky for me your sister was overdue by almost a month and the birth itself killed Celeste. Otherwise I would have had to use a serrated knife to...I need not be so graphic you get the picture."
"You aren't my mother?" Sibylline cried.
"Try listening for a change Sibylline. Neither of you two girls listen; it has to be from Celeste. She was a bad listener too. I am not your mother. I killed the stupid simpleton. She reminds me of you, Sibylline .Celeste was a cow; easily fooled."
"I don't understand," Sibylline cried.
"I shouldn't have dropped you on your head as a baby."

Sibylline stared at her like she never seen her before.

"Don't you look at me like that Sibylline. I did what needed to be done. I could have snuffed out your life but I showed compassion. As Celeste lay dying she requested that I call the babe Sibylline. I'm not heartless I conceded to her wish. I took the babe and presented her as my own. I thought I could be happy as wife, mother, and consort. Did I not mother you Sibylline?"

"You cruel evil witch; how could you say this to Sibylline. You've raised her as your daughter," I spat.

"Ah and now we've come to the cusp of the matter. I am a witch. I gave up on my birthright for fifteen years to become subservient to two nasty little girls and a foolish trusting old man, but no more. I shall not give up what I have fought so hard to keep. I shall reign over Umbria not either of you two brats, or your imbecile father."

"You're a witch?" Sibylline asked incredulously.

"It makes sense she knew how to brew a powerful poison that would kill our father," I answered, "But it won't be so easy for her to rid herself of us."

"I can't use my abilities to rid myself of you two. That would reveal myself too much, but I can do this."

As she said this she pulled a cord that summoned the guards. We heard more fighting then guards burst in.

"Seize them," Helena cried, "They have conspired to kill the King. See, he lies slain."

"Long live the Queen," was the cheer from the guards lips.

Guards then roughly seized us and bound us tightly with chains Helena provided. Albert limped in and I shook my head in warning for him not to do anything.

"Who are you?" Helena asked, but Albert said nothing.

"Answer your Queen," a guard demanded hitting Albert in the stomach.

Albert bravely didn't make a sound.

"He works for the Beast. He cannot speak. The Beast has made him mute," I commented.
"Mute? Hit him again," Helena bade the guard.

Albert made no sound.

"How does he communicate?" Helena demanded.
"He does not. The Beast will miss him you must let him go, or he will come looking for him," I answered.
"Why would you tell me this? Do you not want to be saved by the Beast?"
"I barely escaped from the Beast, obviously he sent this man to retrieve me. I would rather die than go back to him."
"Then so you shall. You and your sister shall linger in our dungeons until the public trial where you will be hanged for poisoning your father."

Sibylline gasped and cried.

"It will be alright Sibylline," I exclaimed trying to comfort my sister.
"Take them away now and release the Beast's pet. I wouldn't want to anger him."

We were escorted to the dungeon. Sibylline was placed in the cell next to mine and I heard her soft cries.

"We'll get out of this Sibylline," I promised her.
It was then I heard a small voice, "Is that you miss? My princess I knew you'd save me."
"I'm sorry Anna. I fear I have trapped us both, but my darling Beast will come. Albert has gone for him."
I only hoped that I had told her the truth and that Albert would be able to get back to Barry. I knew that if Barry knew the situation he would rescue us.

~0~

A fortnight passed and there was no sign of Barry. I worried that Albert had not reached Barry. Had Helena sent someone after Albert? I asked the guard whom I had become friendly with when he came with my nightly bread and water whether there was a male prisoner brought in? He told me no and I believed him.

"Cecilia we're doomed aren't we? No one will save us."
"My Beast will come," I insisted, "But there is no reason why we can't try to free ourselves as well." I told my sister through the hole in the wall.
 "How?" Sibylline asked.
"We dig at our wall. Do you still have that thick silver barrette holding your hair?"
"Yes, Cecilia."
"Remove it and use the tip to dig at the back of your cell. That wall should take us to the outside stairs. Once there we can get outside," I explained.
 "But what about you?"
"I will dig a hole between us and help you once I'm through."
"My body maybe flaccid; but I am agile still. I can help too, there's a hole in the wall between Sibylline and I as well. I'll dig and reach you both," Anna chimed in.
"Thank you Anna, with your help we'll get out of here," I answered.
"This is really hard Cecilia. My fingers are raw already," complained Sibylline.
"Sibylline, I know this is difficult, but in two weeks if we aren't out of here they'll string us up by our necks."
"They'll really kill us Cecilia? But we're royalty," Sibylline protested.
"Little sister, she killed our parents, do you think she'd hesitate to kill us? She'll poison the people against us."
"I'll dig at the wall, but hurry and join me."

"Make sure you both dig when the guard isn't here and put the remains of the wall in a dark corner. If they catch on that we're escaping they may take other measures to keep us," I expounded.

We continued to dig at the walls. Stone crumbled at each of our feet and we hid as many pieces as we could in the dark corners of our cells. After three days I broke through the wall into my sister's cell. It had been made easier by an existing small hole. Anna joined us a day later. We were almost through the wall to the stairs when like a phantom, a man came into the dungeons. He almost caught us digging in Sibylline's cell. We scurried trying to find a way to appear normal and not have him notice the gaping hole and to get back to our own cells.

He strode like a soldier as he walked in. The man was very tall and very skinny and had long dark hair pulled back in a ponytail at his nape.

"Princess Sibylline," the young man began.

Hearing his croaking voice, I realized that he was younger than I thought. He was probably closer to Sibylline's age of sixteen rather than my age of nineteen which had made me an old maid before my marriage to Barry.

"Eric?" Sibylline answered surprised.

 No one existed in his eyes but my sister.

"I've come to rescue you. They mean to hang you at dawn tomorrow."
 "Oh, Eric, what about your father won't he hate you?"
"My father has chosen his side and I've chosen mine."
"But he's the captain of the guard."

"I don't care I love you. I have a sword. See?" Eric cried brandishing it, "We can escape and flee the country."
"How could you think I would escape without my sister?"
"But she killed your father," Eric protested.
"No, she didn't. Helena killed my father. Did you know she's a witch?"
 "Helena but she's your mother."
"She's not my mother she took me from Celeste before she killed her."
"Then she is a witch? A white or black one?"
"Are you always so foolish young man?" Anna asked, "Helena used poisoner skills to kill the King. She's a black witch."
 "Do not speak to me of sorceresses, witch," protested Eric.
"She's not a witch Eric," Sibylline protested.
"You're wasting time arguing. We need to escape now. Can we trust him Sibylline?" I asked.
"Yes."
"Eric we have an escape route will you help us?"
"If what Sibylline says is true, then you are my true Queen Cecilia. I owe you my allegiance and my sword is yours, my lady," Eric cried.

Eric helped us through the hole even making it bigger with his sword. We escaped up the stairs where he bade us wait until a guard had passed. Once we got outside Eric found three horses and brought them to us.

"You'll ride with me Sibylline. We need to go the kingdom of Apricitas and ask for help. It's a day's ride, just past the Beast territory; but don't worry I'll keep you safe. Do you think you can ride that far Sibylline?" Eric demanded.
"With you by my side I can handle anything Eric."
"And you my Queen and your servant? Can you manage?"
"We can, now lead on Eric," I answered mounting a horse.

Eric placed Sibylline sideways in front of him and Anna quickly mounted the last horse. Guards were posted just outside the dungeon but we managed to sneak past the guards, with no blood shed, and went into the forest near the castle avoiding the village. The forest was dark and every noise startled Sibylline; but as night began to fall I saw Barry's castle before me. What had kept him from coming to me? Had something happened to him?

"We will shelter here overnight," I commanded.
"But this is the Beast's home," protested Eric.
"No. this is also my home and I am the Beast's wife. He will not harm us," I confessed to them all.
"She's the Beast's wife? Then she too is a witch, for she has tamed a fierce animal," Eric announced.
"Must you be so backward Eric? My sister obviously used her charm and talents to tame the Beast. She is not a witch, but your sovereign Queen you owe your allegiance to her." scolded Sibylline.
"I am sorry my beloved, Sibylline. Of course you are correct," Eric responded then turning to me and getting on bended knee, he apologized, "Forgive me my queen. I have pledge my fealty to you, Queen Cecilia. You could have me killed for doubting you."

I wanted to scold him for not addressing my sister as Princess; but instead I just accepted his apology and we entered the castle. After a few minutes Agnes appeared without Albert.

"Where is my husband?" I asked.

"Men came in the middle of the night a month ago and stole the Beast away. He hid me and then went to face them. I watched through a peep hole in the wall from the garbage room, as he fought the men. On stole up behind him as if he knew him and then reaching over as if to pat him on the shoulder he grabbed him from behind and put a cloth over his face. You wouldn't have believed it mistress the beast dropped like a stone, he did."

"Then what happened?" I demanded to know.

"They took him and put him in a fine coach, that bear the emblem of Apricitas' flags."

"That makes no sense. A lie told by that evil woman, Helena must have made them seize him," I cried.

"Yes, mistress. I understand that your evil stepmother has slandered your sister and you and condemned you to die for the murder she has wrought. What shall we do, my queen?"

"It is imperative that I go to Apricitas and demand that they surrender my husband, or start a war. Then once my husband is well, then and only then we shall march on Umbria and take back my kingdom with their help."

"You are wise my Queen. The master made a great choice in you. When do we leave, my Queen?"

"We shall depart in five hours' time, when the sun arises."

~0~

A s the morning sun began to arise we had been on the road for an hour. Time went fast and by noon we were at the castle gates of Apricitas. It was then that I found out Agnes was a white witch as she glamoured our coach to appear gilded with gold and as if many soldiers road with me.

I was greeted with fanfare and ushered into the King's ceremonial great hall. As I looked around I saw the walls were stone, but tapestries beautiful and haunting showed battle scenes throughout the centuries. The King though he wore a crown, bore simple clothes though well-made and adorned with silver threads. He was as tall as my Barry and his hair though streaked with gray, had the same shade of red in it I had seen in Barry's. Were all the men in Apricitas redheaded? I wondered as I noted the aide du camp also had a shock of red hair.

The King seemed surprised as his aide whispered in his ear and he took stock of me.

"You claim you are Queen Cecilia of Umbria? And the young woman at the back with the young guard is Princess Sibylline? "
"I am Queen Cecilia, and this is my sister Princess Sibylline," I declared.
"I thought you both confined to dungeons in Umbria, ready to face the gallows."
"My step-mother, the evil Helena Borgia believed that so too."
"You call her evil, but did you not both poison your own father?"

"How dare you slander us, we did not kill our father whom we loved. I was not even in the castle when he was poisoned and my sister had no part in it."

"Then who poisoned my dear friend George, King of Umbria?"

"Helena Borgia schemed and murdered my mother Cecilia to become consort to the King but she wasn't satisfied with that ...no she wanted to be Queen so she slowly poisoned my father and then blamed my sister, and my maid Anna for her crime."

"Do you have proof of this?"

"I have only my word and the body of my mother in her crypt. Helena has committed a grave crime against the people of Umbria and I would beg your help to make this right. But first I beg you to give my husband back."

"I warned your father Helena was capable of this. Wait a minute; you want me to give you back your husband? Who is your husband?"

Loud noises and banging in the outer hall interrupted our conversation.

"Sire you are urgently wanted in the hall," his aide said as another servant whispered in the aides ear.

"Forgive me Queen Cecilia we will continue this conversation when I return. In the meantime my servants we'll serve you and your sister and servants refreshments," King Alfred explained.

"That went well," Sibylline responded as the King left the great hall but I heard a voice outside that I wanted to hear clearer.

I begged Sibylline's silence as I crept to the door to listen but could hear nothing. I tried to open the door but could get no traction. Just as I gave up the King came back in the hall and all was quiet outside it. The King had barely sat on his throne when the doors burst open and a tall man strode in yelling, "I'm not done Father. You must listen to me, I must leave now, my wife may need me."

I looked at the man with shock as his eyes met mine.

"Barry," I whispered.

"You know my son, Edward?" asked King Alfred.

"Edward? Your name is Edward and you're the King's son?" I asked.

"Of course he is, my son's name is Prince Edward Barrett Alfred James."

"Cecilia, oh Cecilia, you are more beautiful then I dreamed," Barry claimed picking me up and twirling me around.

"Why did they take you by force? Wait you can see? How?"

"Yes, Cecilia, I can see but only when I am close up to people. Father's people took me and brought me to his doctor. There the doctor performed surgeries that gave me the ability to see."

"Not without a little fight from my boy. They had to chloroform him," laughed King Alfred.

"That's true. I woke up some days after the surgeries to light and then faces."

"Surgeries?"

"The doctor performed many surgeries on my eyes. I can see now. Father's doctor says it will get better and that I may be able to see as other people in a few weeks."

"You'll be able to see? Oh, Barry that's wonderful." I cried kissing him.

At that moment it was if the world disappeared and we were alone. Barry kissed me back passionately and declared, "I am so glad you're here. Father and his troops have been guarding me day and night and wouldn't let me come to you. I worried that something had happened to you. How did you find me?"

"Agnes told me of the troops that took you in the middle of the night."

"And you came to save me?"

"Yes, and to get help for Umbria."

"What has happened in Umbria? Father said your father was hearty and hale."

"Your father lied. Helena killed him and blamed my sister. Agnes and I for his death, we were to hang on the gallows, until Eric helped us escape," I replied pointing out Eric.

"Then I owe Sir Eric, a great debt. Thank you, Sir Eric."

"I'm just Eric, sire."

"I daub you, Sir Eric then," Barry said grabbing a sword and gently touching Eric's shoulders.

He then turned to the King with anger in his voice, "How could you lie to me father?"

"The doctor said you needed no stress, so the operations would work and you seemed to care so much about the kingdom of Umbria, so forgive me, I lied."

"Of course I cared about the kingdom of Umbria I told you the woman I love was there and I must get to her."

"Who is this woman you love so much? And if you love her so much why were you so glad to see Cecilia?" the looking at Barry and then he answered his own question "Oh..."

"This is my wife, Cecilia Elizabeth Maria Alexandria Celeste, of the house of Attlee, formerly of the house of Sinclair, father."

"Cecilia is your wife? George would love this. He always wanted me to introduce you to Princess Cecilia now Queen Cecilia."

"Did you call her Queen?" asked Barry.

"With her father and her brothers now deceased, Cecilia is the legitimate ruler of Umbria." then turning to me he walked over to me and kissed me gently on the cheek, "Welcome to the family my dear. Call me father."

"Thank you father," I answered, "My sister and my maids, Anna and Agnes need rest, can they shelter here?"

"We would be honoured," King Alfred answered.

"But where is Agnes' husband, Albert? He is Barry's manservant."

"Albert has been restricted to quarters. He tried to move Barry out of the castle," the aide answered.

"We will need Albert to help take back Umbria," I demanded.

"Bring the boy here, Tell him his sire demands his presence as does his Prince now King of Umbria with Queen Cecilia," King Alfred commanded.

"Yes, sire," his aide answered.

"The first order of business is to take back Umbria. Summon the captain of the guard," commanded the king of his guard.

"Yes, sire."

"And I shall lead them," Barry claimed.

"Son, you are barely healed you've had four operations in the last month. Heed your doctor."

"My doctor says I heal. I will protect my eyes with the special glasses you had made for me. But I must help my wife take back her kingdom."

"He is correct. He must lead the charge for he is their sovereign, now my consort." I insisted.

"Very well, I can see you cannot be persuaded. You are too like your father. Your mother, God rest her soul, would be proud of you for marrying Cecilia and fighting for her, so how can I do any less? I shall follow by your side."

"Please Queen Cecilia, may I go too?" Eric asked kneeling before her.

"I am giving you a task much greater. I need someone to protect and guard my sister from any results of the battle. For if we de she will be queen. Will you pledge to do this?"

"I will my Queen!" Eric answered proudly.

"Well done my queen," Barry whispered to me.

"Sire?" the captain of the guards said kneeling before King Alfred.

"Summon a great army we go against Helena Borgia, the poisoner and a black witch of Umbria. She shall rue the day she has harmed kin to the house of Attlee."

~0~

W e road all day and the village was easily taken. All that did not swear allegiance to me were killed. I felt bad about the carnage, but I knew it was necessary. We could leave no people loyal to Helena. We neared the castle at twilight. They were ready for us and fired upon us. It was then that I found out my husband's family's true secret they were Wizards of white magic. With a wave of his hand King Alfred was able to obscure their vision of us. A strange white mist came across us and in their eyes they saw nothing it was as if we were ghosts.

Barry took me into the castle and into the inner sanctum of Helena, along with a number of troops and no one stopped us they couldn't see us. I reappeared to gasps and then laughter from Helena. The troops and Barry remained invisible.

"Tricks, Cecilia? I am much more powerful then these petty little magic deceptions," Helena quipped.
"Are you Helena? You are a poisoner and have sinned greatly against the people of Umbria," I shouted so all could hear.
"I have sinned. Your family have used the people for years. They know what to expect from me. I reward loyalty do you?" Helena cried indignantly.
"My people are my family. They know that I will look after them and see that they have work to do, food to eat and a roof over their heads. Can you provide the same?"
"Their job is to look after my wants and needs not the other way around. You came here alone? You were always so foolish and trusting Cecilia. There can be only one Queen. Seize her," Helena commanded.

Barry reappeared along with all the troops. He took his glasses off that kept his eyes safe from glare and his eyes glowed like fire. And red fur appeared all over his body. He looked like the Beast they called him. If I hadn't known the gentleness of Barry I would be afraid.

"Is that supposed to frighten me? So you're the Beast? I'm afraid," Helena cried, covering her mouth and then spoiling it all with a hearty laugh saying, "Perhaps I shall have a Beast head for my castle wall."
"Helena Borgia you have one last chance to admit your crimes and save your life."

Helena volleyed fire at us but Barry stopped it as he lifted one finger.

"Well played Beast. You are powerful, but I am more powerful then you," Helena claimed.

Helena then muttered under her breath and a mist started coming our way. Barry chanted and a bubble appeared around us and the troops and anyone who had moved closer to us. People two feet from Helena dropped like flies coughing and sputtering. Barry took pity on those and cleared the air around them placing them also in a bubble where they could breathe.

"Damn it backfired how did you do that? No matter, I am powerful and I shall defeat you both."
"Will you Helena Borgia?"
"Why do you keep saying her full name," I whispered.

I heard to my surprise an answer not in words but within my head, "Names are power. I exert my power over her. She does not know mine and cannot exert this over me."

Helena tried to send lightning bolts our way but Barry stopped those too. Helena looked frustrated and angry. Then she smiled sweetly to my surprise and I knew she'd found another plan.

"Why do you protect Cecilia? She is dull and barely pretty. She is also a sheltered virgin. I could offer you so much more," Helena offered.
"You have nothing I want you are shallow and have no beauty."
"Are you blind? I am beautiful and I please any man. How do you think I survived so long, with that ugly old man, the King?"
"Don't listen to her," I cautioned.
"Some would say you were beautiful, but I see only the ugliness within. You are an infestation that takes over and ruins the harvest."
"You, the ugliest creature I've ever seen dare to speak this way to me?"
"He is more beautiful inside and out then you could ever be," I defended.
"You do have some charms. You've tamed the Beast. Isn't that cute you pretend to love the Beast. I underestimated you."
"Shut-up, Helena."
"You were supposed to die at his feet. Now he'll die too and you'll still die at his feet but the Beast will die with a broken heart. You poor dear, Beastie."
"Admit your crimes Helena Borgia," Barry demanded again.
"Fine, I'll confess to necessary killings, but there was no crime, only a gift to the kingdom of Umbria. Where shall I start? I tortured and killed Maria Celeste, Queen of Umbria. I took her baby and then her life. But she whined, and she was flabby, making her a woman unfit to be a queen.
"She was pregnant, not flabby," I protested.

"Piffle, I actually saved the kingdom by doing away with her. I became Queen and helped that snivelling George govern. For years I had to being subjected to the King's evening ministrations. Only my nightly romps with Victor here saved me from suicide. Victor shall be my consort. Won't you my dear, Victor?"

"Yes, my queen."

"Victor, your son Eric has joined us. He loves Sibylline. Join us too," I begged.

"I cannot my loyalty is with my queen, Queen Helena."

"Cecilia is your true Queen you owe allegiance only to her," Barry insisted.

"Shall I slit his throat in front of you and show you how much he's under my command? Shall I allow you to smell the stench of his blood as it spurts from his neck?" Helena asked us then turning to Victor she demanded, "Victor show me your throat."

"Yes, my queen," Victor responded, offering his throat.

"You would harm someone so loyal to you? You're callous and cold -blooded."

"Callous? I'll show you cold-blooded Cecilia. I could slit your sister's throat wherever she is from here."

"You wouldn't!"

"Cecilia, I won't do it now, but remember I could. I powered all my attention into raising you two girls and where did that get me?"

"It got you love and affection from my entire family but that wasn't good enough was it Helena?" I stated.

"Love and affection? Is that what you called it? There was none of that, only a cabal against me."

"Confess your crimes Helena Borgia," Barry demanded again.

"Crimes, what crimes? Why yes, I did try to poison my stepdaughters, Cecilia and Sibylline. They loved their father and would have wanted to be with him. However they didn't like the taste and would swallow it. Nasty, ungrateful brats!"

I couldn't believe it she'd try to poison my sister and I too. I shouldn't be so surprised since she gave me to the Beast, but somehow I was.

"She's up to something. Don't listen to her," I cried.
"But you understand that don't you dear Beast. These two girls have used you. Cecilia doesn't love you. How could she? You're an ugly beast!"

Barry looked like he believed her and I became worried. Barry however continued to listen to her. Helena's voice had changed to a sing-song quality as she droned on. I had to stop her before she mesmerized him. I stepped forward to shake her and she volleyed a fireball at me. Barry at the last second noticed it and turned it back on Helena.

"A curse I place upon your head, a million times worse instead, unless your true love proves her devotion, then you shall be trapped in your own body with no emotion." Helena croaked out and then died.

Barry lay still beside me. At first I was sure he was dead. I touched his face and it felt warm. Surely he was still alive? Tears fell from my eyes and I tenderly kissed his lips. I loved Barry with all my heart. Why wasn't that enough to break Helena's curse?

"I love you. I would give my throne for you, anything for you my beloved, Teddy Bear," I declared willing him to keep breathing and wake up for me.
"But you don't have to my love. Your kisses and declarations of devotion have beaten Helena's curse," Barry answered his eyes meeting mine, "I would marry you all over again my love."
"What a wonderful idea," declared King Alfred, "Our two kingdoms shall be united in t's love for Queen Cecilia and Prince Edward."

We were married again in front of all our peoples and the kingdoms of Umbria and Apricitas were joined as one. The people chose a name more befitting for our homeland. We became Lux the Latin word for light. Or kingdom flourished and in time Barry and I welcomed the addition of our daughter Devorah and our son Ezekiel.

Sibylline and Eric were married and they too enjoyed bliss, as Sibylline bore cousins for Devorah and Ezekiel of the same age and gender. Eric was elevated to knight of the realm.

The Beast retired, to become a father and a King, and to help me govern and keep our people safe. Our kingdoms now bathed in sunshine, happiness and song, all because my stepmother feared the beast; and I met fell in love and married my beast, Bear Brave, the prince of Apricitas my future consort and the future king of Umbria. I had achieved the greatest end to my fairy-tale after all for we were living happily ever after.

~0~

The Legend of Maes Gwyddno

In the valley stood Cantre'r Gwaelod in the county of Dyfed, west Wales surrounded by forest, to keep out the sea. In a nearby kingdom of Helig ap Glanawg, King Carwyn's wife Neirin gave birth to a maiden Mererid. Neirin died shortly after. The kingdom fell into mourning and King Carwyn called on three of Neirin's sisters, Blodeuwedd, Berwyn, and Brynmoor to look after and raise the heir to the kingdom. What King Carwyn didn't know Neirin had four sisters, one of them condemned to live in the forest that kept the waters from Cantre'r Gwaelod but also from King Carwyn's kingdom of Helig ap Glanawg. Neirin's sister, Bran could leave the forest from time to time but must return when it rained or stormed.

The three sisters held a christening for Mererid and bestowed gifts upon the little princess. Blodeuwedd gave her the gift of beauty. Berwyn gave her the gift of lyrical speech. Brynmoor gave her the gift to find true love. Bran burst in and acted like she had been invited bestowing on Mererid a voice that could sing like an angels, but in anger destroy. Then Bran laughed and left returning to her forest.

The three aunts tried to keep Mererid from ever singing a note but that proved impossible, so they cautioned Mererid to never sing in anger, lest the gift be realized. Mererid grew older and more beautiful every day as she reached her sixteenth birthday her father cast his eyes on the nearby kingdom's sons, Prince Seithenyn and Prince Dewi. Their father the great King Gwynddo had built a dyke to also protect the fertile grounds of the city and surrounding areas from the sea's reach. Members of the royal family and some upper echelon government members were tasked with guarding the barrier and letting in small waters from time to time to save the valley. This dyke also kept the waters from Helig ap Glanawg, so King Carwyn held them in great esteem. Since Prince Seithenyn was the older prince it was declared that Mererid would marry him and unite the kingdoms.

When Prince Seithenyn saw the lovely Mererid, her hair shining and glimmering like fine red cedar; her eyes doe like, the colour of a fawn, he fell deeply in love. He gave up the drink that plagued him and became the prince his father had always wanted. King Gwynddo grew happy and knew that Prince Seithenyn could be the prince now he always aspired to be. Mereid would be the making of his son.

Mererid was not in love with him, but she felt sure love would come so she agreed and the papers were signed. Two weeks to the wedding Mererid met Prince Dewi. Though he looked like his brother with his dark raven coloured hair and blue eyes, Mererid saw a kindness and strength of character lacking in his brother. Prince Dewi too fell hard for Mererid. The two went to their father's and begged to be released to marry each other and the two kings refused. The wedding what forth and though Mererid did not agree, they were declared wed. Prince Seithenyn looked forward to the marriage bed and although he pledged not to drink again when offered toasts to his wedding, he could not refuse.

Mererid thought Prince Seithenyn a beast, and spoke with Prince Dewi of her plan to retain the love of Mererid and Dewi. Prince Seithenyn saw them whispering and grew angry, but he knew Mererid would soon be his forever more tonight, one more ale would not go to waste.
 He tipped the ale up to his mouth and then had some more. Prince Seithenyn got so drunk when he entered the bedroom he passed out. Mererid had hoped this would happen and she placed the pig's blood on the mattress to show he had taken her virginity. She knew he would leave early in the morning to do his duty to watch the dyke. Prince Seithenyn left thinking he had taken his bride, but vowed to do better this evening without the drink to cloud his mind and memories.

As soon as he left Mererid ushered Prince Dewi in to help her pack, for they vowed to run away together. He touched her hand and before she knew it they lay naked side by side wrapped in each other's arms making sweet love. Time had no meaning as they wiled the hours away. Before long the sun started to go down and they realized they'd been together for hours. The door opened and Prince Seithenyn walked in finding them together he flew into a rage. He beat his brother to a pulp and dragged him to the dyke where he threw Prince Dewi into the drainage ditch where Prince Dewi drowned. Mererid lost all reason and as Prince Seithenyn began to drink getting roaring drunk and laughing about how he killed his brother. Mererid's anger grew until she had to let it out. She opened her mouth and sang in anger.

Winds roared and still she sang on. Water lifted right over the forest and still Mererid sang on. Gale winds roared, winding ripping her from her feet and still she sang in grief and anger. Soon the dyke broke and water poured into both kingdoms. The people fled as best they could, but Prince Seithenyn stood raptured in Mererid's song and watched at the highest point. Mererid sang loudly, as the forest and the kingdoms covered in water. Soon the water slurped and lapped at their feet, then their waists, but still Mererid continued until they were covered completely and knew no more. In the legend of Cantre'r Gwaelod that Prince Seithenyn lies forever blamed for drinking heavily and opening the dyke, when true lovers crossed was the cause.

This is all in the writer's imagination, but there is a legend of Maes Gwyddno where Prince Seithenyn's drunkenness is to blame. They believe he opened the dyke and let the water in that covered the city. Recently, in the storms, they found parts of the petrified forest showing above the water off the coast off Cardigan Bay Wales.

~0~

The Fairy Stones

My name is Elizabeth Yarborough. When I was little, I wished for a world where I didn't have to live the life of a pampered society daughter, or wife. I'd seen what had happened to my sister after her marriage, and I wanted none of it. But opportunity to escape is not given to daughters. We are never allowed out alone, so escape is futile.

We are pampered taught the fine arts of how to please our husbands, then sold to the highest bidder as my sister had been. But escape is what I wanted. I wanted more then to be a wife and mother. I wanted to see the world and most of all I wanted to write. I hated the restrictions of this society and yet I was glad I did not have to labor as the servants did.

It neared my fifteenth birthday and already my mother plotted to find my husband. My mother wanted the highest in the land for my husband, someone full of pocket and high in title. My father who loved me deeply wanted me to be happy. Father was sweet and kind but also easily thwarted by my much stronger willed mother. He wished for a husband who would treat me well but I knew she would always win. . My father asked if I wanted something special for my last birthday with him. I chose a trip to visit my grandparent's in the Highlands, but I knew mother would cancel my wish. Mother hated the place of her birth Mother surprised me however when she agreed. We could go (Father and I) while she would remain behind. I was very afraid that this meant she had found the man of her dreams for me, and was readying him for his agreement to marry me.

My grandfather, my mother's father, was so much different than she. He told me stories of other places and of a woman who led soldiers into battle. His tales had made me happy as a child and had kept me dreaming that there could be another future for me.

So here I am its early May, but the snow lays heavy, in the higher elevations here. Flowers are budding and the grass is growing green, high and long. The rains come but so does the sun which awakens the birds, and the flowers. I yearn to visit the fairy ring Grandfather took me to once when I was five. Yesterday it was raining, today the sun is shining and the dew is drying on the grass, as the sun burns it off. I am up an unheard of time in society circles. It is seven in the morning. Grandfather is up and said to me.

"I knew ye wur th' granddaughter efter mah ain hert. Ye dinnae primp an preen th' wey yer mither does, 'n' ye aren't feart tae bide yer lee."

"Thank you Grandfather," I answered not sure where he was going with this.

"Wid ye be up tae gaun tae th' fairy ring wi' me this mornin'?"

"Aye I would Grandfather," I answered eagerly. My heart's desire and he was offering it to me almost like he could read my mind. For a moment I wondered if he could read my mind.

"Wid ye lik' tae mooch a pair o' breeks 'n' some bits? Yer dress wid be ruined by th' lang grasses 'n mud we mist travel thro' tae git thare."

"What would father say?"

"Do ye pure care whit yer Faither micht say. We kin keep it a secret atween us. You kin lea a hain dress in th' shed thare 'n' chaynge whin we come back."

"I love Father but he would frown on such clothing. Thank you Grandfather." I said hugging him and he sent a servant to fetch the clothes I would wear.

"Thae ur yer Uncle Jaime's auld claes frae whin he wis a wee jimmy bit thay shuid fit ye."

"Uncle Jaime, who is Uncle Jaime?" I asked, but no answer came.

Grandfather gave orders to the servants should Father wake before his customary noon arising that they were to say we'd travel to a neighbours for lunch and would be back by three pm. That gave us a whole day to spend at the fairy stones. I was so excited.

"Ye'v grown intae a bonny lassie bit ah fear ye'll nae be satisfied wi' th' usual husband. You need someone wha wull let ye be th' body yer. Ah huv tried tae mak' yer mither 'n' faither listen bit thay hear me nae. Sae th'day wull pat they cares aside 'n' ye shall gilravage yer day at th' stanes."
"I will enjoy my Day .Thank you Grandfather."

We traipsed through long wet grasses and over hills and marsh and around the bog until we almost reached the fairy stones. They gleamed brightly in the sunlight and I smiled as I saw them. I could almost hear them singing a song to me. a song with such longing that I ran the short distance left to them and their standing in the stones I felt a peace come over me that I didn't know I had longed for.

"Ah brought th' lassie as promised. She haes reached her sixteenth birthday. Noo ah huv fulfilled oor bargain. Will ye let mah son gang?"

Had the one person I trusted betrayed me? Who was he fulfilling a bargain with? I saw no one. What did this mean for me? Was the grandfather I trusted giving me away to someone? And of what son did he speak as far as I knew he only had one child, my mother. Except a short time ago he had mentioned an Uncle Jaime. I thought maybe this had been his brother but now...I must flee and protect myself.

I stepped forward as if to leave the singing stones and a light enveloped me. I felt dizzy and my head pulsed to the music. My skin felt like elastic stretched beyond its limit. When I thought I could bare the light and sound no more I closed my eyes and was soon unconscious.

~0~

I opened my eyes slowly a thumping pain still behind my crinkled eyes. A heavy fog was everywhere and I couldn't see or navigate two feet in front of me.

'Ere noo wha urr ye lassie?" a strange voice at my elbow demanded.

"Who are you?" I demanded frightened but hiding it I could now see the six foot tall man with a shock of red curly hair to his shoulders. His eyebrows were also thick and fuller then most and red over bright eyes the colour of my favourite emerald necklace,

"A'm Jaime Ferguson."

"Are you the Jaime grandfather pleaded for the return of?"

"Is yer Grandfather a rid headed Ferguson wha doesn't blither a lot?"

"Yes, I guess that's Grandfather."

"Then a'm Jaime. Would ye be Elizabeth?"

"How do you know my name?"

"I ken you."

"But how do you know me?" I asked but he didn't answer.

"Mah faither main hae begged th' fairies fur mah return. Ah huv bin 'ere alang time, whit year is it?"

"It is the year of our lord eighteen hundred and fifty two."

"Tis bin sixteen years 'ere in this netherworld and den in dis fog. I cannae hawp tis bin sae lang. Ah cam athwart oan a body ay th' days, 'at th' spirit warld considers sacred, a leap day in 1836."

"You are claiming you've been here at the fairy stones, in the fog for sixteen years? You've been there since the year of our lord eighteen hundred and thirty six? "

"Dae ye ken whaur yer Elizabeth?

"I am in the circle of the fairy stones," I answered.

"Aye ye wur in th' fairy stanes bit nae anymair."

"Then where are we?"

"We ur in th' netherworld, halfway atween th' real world 'n' th' fairy world. Time moves fest in th' netherworld.yoo coods hae aw ready bin haur almost a year."

"Nonsense what has bewitched you?"

"You hawp in witches bit nae th' fairies?"

"I believe in only what my eyes tell me," I answered annoyed.

"Is this a normal rowk? 'n' whit dae yer een tell ye"

"My eyes tell me it's a thick fog that makes it hard to see." I insisted, but somehow I was worried. The fog was thicker then I had ever seen it, and where was Grandfather? He wouldn't have just left us. Where had Uncle Jaime been that Grandfather thought he must sacrifice me?"

"Whaur is ma sister?"

"My mother?"

"She isnae yer mither."

"Of course she's my mother," I answered angrily.

"She's mah sister 'n' she teuk you."

"I don't understand."

"Ah cam tae th' stanes 'n' met a maiden, 'n' we made a baby. Her faither wis heich in th' fairy court 'n' he wis angered that mah wean wis noo sharing his bloodline. He cast me intae th' netherworld 'n' then tae punish mah fair Eolande. Fur yer birth he cast th' wean oot. Ah hae bin haur in thes fog since yer birth."

"You are saying you had a child with a fairy named Eolande, but they gave that child away and placed you here this place you call the Netherworld?"

"Aye bit ye dinnae ken. Mah sister wis barren 'n' she cam tae th' fairy stanes tae beg fur a boon o' a child. Eolande's faither thought it a fit punishment fur me 'n' Eolande tae lose oor wean tae th' sister ah loathe."

I was stunned did this explain my mother's coolness toward me? She wanted a child but she didn't understand me. But what of the man who had always been my father? He loved me, I know he did. This couldn't be true. No one truly believed in fairies. They were just tales told to the gullible. Weren't they? I starred around I still couldn't see anything around myself but heavy air and fog. I became frightened.

"A've frightened you. I'm sorry. You ur a wean o' th' fairies as weel as mine. They dae nae listen tae mah plea fur release bit thay wilnae keep ye a prisoner."
"But there's no one here. It's like we are in a land of nothingness."
"Aye tis bit thay come wance a day tae lea mah fairn, 'n' thay wull tak' mah plea tae thair King, or mah name isn't Jaime Ferguson."
"Have we long to wait?" I asked beginning to believe him.
"Not long., thay come soon." He said turning as if he heard something I didn't in the fog.

A light burnt away the fog as if a door had opened. A figure appeared light from within as well as without. She was beautiful to behold her hair like mine gleamed like spun gold in the light. Her eyes were the same odd violet colour as mine. She spotted me and her eyed grew wide as saucers. She blinked away unshed tears and walked arms out stretched towards me. I wondered who she could be and then I saw Jaime's face. He looked like man who had seen steak after going hungry. She pulled both our hands and we stepped into a land like I'd never seen before. It was lush and lovely. Greenery was everywhere and flowers. I felt a peace and contentment come over me. Then a figure stepped in front of us on our path and I could sense the fairy who greeted was frightened. I too became frightened but Jaime, the man who claimed he was my father, stepped in front of us in a stance of protection.

The man who stood before us was tall with hair as black as midnight .His hair was curly and tight to his head like he kept it clipped short. His eyes were a piercing sky blue and he appeared no more than twenty five years old.

"Yer th' half-ling that wis taken frae us by him," the man yelled grabbing Jaime.
"I am beginning to believe that I might be a half-ling, but Jaime didn't take me, and I wish everyone didn't speak with such a thick Celtic accent. It makes it hard to understand you all," I protested.

To my surprise all of a sudden their language was clear as if they were speaking the King's English.

"If this is the Jaime ye speak of he took you from your mother and gave you away. Is that not correct Eolande?"

Before my newfound mother could answer a man large and overbearing reached out and pulled her to his side.
"Tell the truth daughter. Tell them how the deviant snatched the babe from yer arms after she was born." Her father said as he pinched her arm.
"No Sire it's not so. This was a story conceived by my father that protected himself from your Father's wrath."

I was amazed at the courage of my newfound mother; for she stood up to her King and told the truth. As I thought this however her father struck her across the face and said,
"You would lie to your King, daughter? "
"Nae."
"Hefeydd you dare to lie again to your King? Do you think yourself beyond punishment?"

"My King, I only sought to save our world from the taint she brought to it."

"You lied to your King, my father. You kept that lie for sixteen years. My Father punished the other worlder and ye said nothing," Eolande screamed.

"Father do not protect me," woman said appearing out of almost nowhere. She was tall and thin her hair was red and ringlets cascaded down her back covering tiny wings. She wore a pale mint green dress.

"You, of course, it was you Rhiannon. Ye took my child and gave her away like she was a kitten," Eolande shouted grabbing a handful of her sister's hair.

"I did the right thing Eolande. You know I did. This wasn't a trivial matter sister," Rhiannon responded, then as Elonade pulled her hair she said, "That hurts let go of my hair."

"Let go of your sister at once," Hefeydd demanded.

"Eolande you will let yer king handle this," King Fáelán retorted.

"I am your servant King Fáelán and I obey," Eolande replied letting go of Rhiannon's hair.

"What have you to say for yourself Rhiannon?" asked King Fáelán.

"My sister is a harlot. She entices men with her dimples and her smiles and draws them in. She went willingly to the other world years ago and chose this man and hochmagandy took place. She bore a baby that is more human than fairy. I did what was necessary to protect us all."

"You took on what was not your place and you lied to your King. How would you have me punish you Rhiannon?"

"Ah don't know sire."

"Should I let your sister Eolande or your niece decide your punishment?"

Rhiannon didn't answer.

"Take her into custody." King Fáelán said to his guards who promptly did so. "I shall decide her fate tomorrow." Turning to my mother he said "What should I do with the interloper Jaime?"

"Sire my father has been punished. For sixteen years he has been cast in fog. Can he not be set free?" I begged.

"What will you give your King for this boon?"

"Do not promise anything daughter. I can survive in that fog again." Jaime cautioned me.

"Would ye give me this evening? Spend time with me eat, drink and celebrate the festival of Belltaine? Even now my people prepare for the grand feast."

"Why do you call it Belltaine, is it not Beltane?"

"Do ye recognize none of your Celtic roots, or your fairy blood? Even the brute who is your father would call it Bealtaine. Your Aunt Rhiannon has done you a great disservice raising you among the Sassenach."

"Do not insult the people who raised me," I defended my parents.

"You are loyal, but mind what you say about your true family the fairy folk." King Fáelán cautioned, "Come Elizabeth I call ye that as a courtesy though, as that was your fairy name. It's a minuscule thing for your King to ask of you."

"You say that Elizabeth was not my birth name? Then who named me Elizabeth and what was I really called?"

"Elizabeth is not your fairy name. Who would give fairy folk such name?" King Fáelán insisted almost sounding insulted.

I looked at him but he still didn't answer what my fairy name was. He did however look at Eolande.

"I called you Orlagh, after my mother." Eolande answered quietly, "Jaime's sister renamed you Elizabeth."

"Can I call you Orlagh?" King Fáelán asked.

"Do not agree with anything he asks. He's a trickster," Jaime cautioned.

"No you'll call me Elizabeth," I demanded.

"It's not a trick. Come eat drink and be merry Elizabeth Orlagh. Eolande and even the interloper can join us for the feast. Tomorrow will come soon enough for decisions to be made. We will sup and drink of spring's labours and just celebrate," King Fáelán said taking my hand and to my surprise I found myself walking agreeably beside him.

We walked into a land of green lush grass. Trees that hung heavy with fruit as a stream flowed gently through it. We stayed on path that seemed to weave through the entire village. We reached a staging area where two gilded chairs rose above other chairs. One was slightly higher than the other. King Fáelán pulled me up to the slightly lower gilded chair and placed me in it causing gasps from the other fairies there. My parents sat further below Jaime's smile wide as he held my mother's hand.

"Sire she shouldn't sit there. She's a Halfling," protested one of his guards.

"You dare to question me?" King Fáelán demanded his eyes narrowing and even I became frightened. He then turned and smiled at me putting me at ease.

Some fairies danced an intricate dance for their King with ribbons and flowers thrown in the air and all about celebrating the festival of Belltaine. King Fáelán explained the celebrations to me and was an interesting conversationalist. Okay, so it wasn't just his sparkling conversation I enjoyed.

He had a magnetism about him that made me want to spend more time with him and get to know him better. I ate drank and made merry, enjoying the King's company. He handed me grapes and his hand swept my lips. When his hand clasped mine I felt chills and wanted more I wasn't quite sure what. Just to have him near me perhaps. His smile was enchanting and bewitching. I looked at him through my eyelashes as he swooped in for a kiss and wondered, "Oh no, could it be that was he using his fairy abilities on me?"

These thoughts and the kiss were interrupted by the King's guard who exclaimed loudly "Sire they've disappeared."
"Who has disappeared?"
"The interloper and the fairy princess, Eolande."

I was alarmed to realize I hadn't even noticed. What would the King do to my parents?

"I give them amnesty and this is how I am rewarded?" King Fáelán shouted angrily.
"Please, your Majesty. They love one another. Why can't they be together?" I dared to ask.
"Find the interloper and the princess, Eolande and bring them to me."

The King's guard dragged my mother Eolande and my father Jaime letting them stand unchained before the monarch.

"Ye have defied your King. Has hochmagandy teuk place again?" the King asked of my parents.

My mother looked like she would open her mouth; but my father put his hand on her arm and she said nothing.

"We found thaim wit' there clothes oan yer majesty," the guard answered.

"That does negate that we found thaim together," the other guard argued.

"They are in love, show some compassion. Please let them go," I begged running up and throwing my parents behind me.

"You do not command a King," King Fáelán answered.

I looked at him in surprise this didn't even seem the same man I had sat and talked with and yet he looked the same. I was baffled.

"Step forth 'n' take yer punishment," ordered King Fáelán "Or do ye cower behind yer wean?"

Anger so fierce came over me, to my surprise sparks flew out my fingernails. Overhead thunder rumbled and the sky grew dark overhead of me. Yet the sun shone in the rest of the sky. Fairies looked at the sky directly over me, in surprise. Fog then seeped over my parents completely covering them.

Was this my doing? Had I tapped unknown fairy ability? Growing confidence I retorted through clenched teeth. "You will not harm them."

"Harm thaim? Thay have disappeared. How kin I harm thaim? Who has done this? Ah ken Eolande isn't strong enough tae do this."

I couldn't believe the King was unable to see them. I looked behind me. My father Jaime and my mother Eolande were clearly visible to me although fog still surrounded them. My mother smiled and my father put a finger to his lips, as if to say don't give them away.

To my great surprise I could see the King standing behind them, although he was still unable to see them. How did he move so fast? I looked back to see where his guards were and saw him standing behind me. I turned slightly to view both back and front and discovered there were two of him. How did he divide himself in two? I wondered.

"Kellen ah should have known. What have ye done? Where is Eolande and the interloper?" asked the King of his double.
"I have done nae Father. Ye do not give Elizabeth credit."

Father? But this fairy looked exactly like the other even to his age. How could they be father and son?

"Elizabeth is halfling. She could nae have made thaim disappear."
"And yet she did!"
"Robin Goodfellow."
"Yes, sire."
"Can ye tell how fur muckle fairy blood this halfling has?"
"Give me a moment sire tae judge," Robin Goodfellow said staring hard at me.

Robin Goodfellow a short burly unlikely looking fairy stood in front of me and I grew afraid.

"Ah will nae harm ye lassie. I seek tae find oot your lineage with a wave of my hands," Robin said to me as if I'd spoken.

He then waved his arms from the top of my head to the tips of my feet. The first time he looked puzzled as if he had done it incorrectly. The second time he looked completely dumfounded.

"Well Robin?" The King asked.

"It is shocking sire. She is not a *Halfling* at all she is almost a full blooded fairy. How ken that be?"

"How can this be?" asked King Fáelán "Who is th' faither o' Eolonde's wean it's nae the interloper. I go away fur a few weeks n' unknown fairies come home?"

"Father! We agreed you would not tell the subjects." Kellen censored, "As for her parentage, ah think the interloper is her father and has fairy blood."

"Ye think th' interloper is fairy. No we'd have known. As fer the other maiter dae not worry wee jimmy the subjects can know now. There wull be noo war with' elves .King Aelfric haes given me his word."

"We have bin deceived Kellen wis acting as our King," the fairies whispered all around me.

"He is oor King he kin dae as he pleases," answered another and they all then seemed to reluctantly agree.

I was baffled. Kellen had been acting as the King? Had it been Kellen all along?

"I am sorry Elizabeth that I couldn't be honest with you. I spent the day with you. Father left at the beginning before we went to the festival. I switched back with father as the guards came to tell him of your parent's disappearance," Kellen whispered to me as he came to stand beside me.

He looked contrite and I almost felt sorry for him but then I remembered once again his deceit. I frowned at him.

"Who ur yer grandparents?" demanded the King breaking my thoughts.

I scowled at the King, even if I knew I didn't feel like answer him. He had threatened my parents and now he wanted to know my family. Did he seek to harm them too?

"I would ask a boon of you Elizabeth. My father would know who your grandparents are. Could you ask your father his lineage on his mother's side? I will see he harms them not," Kellen whispered.

"You know I can see them?" I whispered back.

"Of course you can. You made them invisible. I can give you my power to speak with them telepathically and then no one can hear," Kellen offered still whispering.

Should I trust him? I wondered. I wanted to trust him but he had pretended to be his father. He smiled at me and my heart turned over. I nodded and I was able to hear and talk to my parents in my mind.

"Daughter ye wish tae ken yer Grandmother's name?" asked my father.

"Yes."

"My mother wis Alvina. She disappeared when ah was a wee jimmy. Mah father said th' fairies took her back."

"The fairies took her back?'

"Aye. Her mother wis took first when Alvina was a baby."

"What was her mother's name?"

"Twas Lorelle."

"Lorelle?"

"Aye, Lorelle was her name. His grandmother Shaylee wis kidnapped by an elf cried Elden and Faither said Lorelle came from an elf 'n' a fairy 'n' wasn't his grandfather's wean at all..But 'twas juist a story."

I was shocked this meant I had human, fairy blood and elfin blood if the story was true.

"Her great-grandmother was Lorelle," Kellan announced. He must have been able to listen into our conversation I surmised.

"Did you say Lorelle, Kellen? Are you sure?" the King demanded.

"Yes,sire," Kellen responded as I glared at him in his betrayal of my trust.

A man dressed in elegant clothing like he was going to a ball, suddenly interrupted the proceedings. His hair was long and black but braided and tied up with a colourful ribbon.

"Tis the Herald," the other fairies cried out.

"Sire, there is a prophecy about the granddaughter of Shaylee," the Herald announced.

"Shaylee? What has Shaylee to do with this once thought Halfling?"

"You know the lineage Father. Lorelle, daughter of Shaylee, shall give birth to a great queen of the fairies."

"You are trying tae tell me that this lassie this fairy we though a Halfling is part of the legend...but wasn't the legend's name Bess?" asked the King

"My nickname is Bess," I answered in a whisper but they heard anyway.

"Tell me the legend now." King Fáelán commanded.

The Herald then began to recite, "*A daughter born of fairies fair,*
A son born of elfin rare,
True love will bloom
As passions zoom
Child of passion
Not fairy, human or elfin
But all three
So shall he be
He will cross the divide

And to his love he will abide
To make a true alliance of elfin,
Fairy and queen.
A child named Bess
We do confess
Will save the fairies
When she marries
From war and doom
When an fairy seeks a boon"

"Nonsense it's just a legend and a coincidence. You will unveil the interloper now girl."
"Have you broken our peace already King Fáelán?" A voice asked interrupting.

I turned to spot a tall man with elfin ears. His hair was long a golden, his eyes a sherry brown. He was surrounded by a crowd of fifty elves with bows and other weapons.

"King Aelfric? Why was I not informed you had arrived?"
"You were too busy thinking up a punishment for my grandchildren," King Aelfric answered drily.
"The peace we brokered has nae bin broken, even by yer presence here with' armed guards," King Fáelán countered.
"Is it not true my grandson Jaime has been a prisoner for sixteen years? And you continue to threaten my grandchildren?"
"The person who held him has been dealt with."
"And yet I find you threatening my grandson and great-granddaughter. This means war."
"Please King Aelfric, we can settle this can we not?" asked Kellen.
"How can we make peace Aelfric?" King Fáelán queried.
"There must be an alliance between our houses."
"An alliance?" King Fáelán asked.
"Aye an alliance, to bind the two houses," King Aelfiric demanded.

"So shall it be so shall it be written," King Fáelán agreed.
"What have they agreed to?" I asked Kellen trying to understand
"They have said ...,"began Kellen
"Kellen will marry you my beloved great granddaughter, Elizabeth Moragh," commanded King Aelfric.
"But I haven't agreed to this." I protested.
"You will!" both Kings responded.

I wanted to flee but where could I go? I didn't know the way out of this land of the fairies. Yet if I refused to marry there would be a war between the fairies and the elves who claimed to be my kin. I was an amateur when it came to politics I knew no way out. Then there was the matter of my parents. they had never nurtured me or raised me but I had grown to care about them.

I would also put them in danger. I was between a rock and a hard spot. Maybe my parents could help me with this?

I looked over at my parents behind me and to my dismay saw that whatever had caused them to be invisible to others had now dissipated. I couldn't leave my parents to the punishment King Fáelán would mete out. I wouldn't ask them to help me decide. I really didn't have any choice but to agree. I opened my mouth to tell them so when I was interrupted.

"I seek a boon for myself 'n' Elizabeth, Father. I ask that we have a week tae get tae each other afore the ceremony."
"Whit say ye Aelfiric. Aye or na?" King Fáelán responded.
"A week to get to know the elfin fairy you'll spend your life with? It seems a fair trade. I shall return in a week's time for the weddings."
"Weddings? I don't ken," King Fáelán asked.
"Aye my grandson shall marry his fairy love."
"I didnae gree tae that."

"My grandson has been grievously wronged, Kept prisoner for sixteen long years would you deny him his heart's desire?"

"Na."

"You will agree it is what I require of the peace treaty," King Aelfric demanded.

"She is fairy she cannae bide in his world 'n' he cannae bide lang here."

"Aye that is why I invite them to live in the elfin world protected from what would harm them both. My great granddaughter Elizabeth can exist in either world so she may remain here."

"If ah must gree then in a week's time ah shall see ye fur th' weddings," conceded King Fáelán.

"Jaime and his fairy Eolonde will come with me for safe keeping and you shall prepare a great feast for the weddings, worthy of elf and fairy union."

"Aye then."

I was happy for my parents they obviously loved one another, after all I was result of their love but they were leaving me alone here. I didn't want to remain here. Could I visit my former parents occasionally if I had to marry Kellen? The afternoon I had spent with Kellen had been fun and even romantic at times but he had lied to me. He pretended to be his father and didn't enlighten me and this was the man (or should I say fairy) I was being forced to marry? At least he had bought me a week to get to know him but could I ever trust him again? I looked sideways at him and some of my mistrust must have shown for he said to me.

"Elizabeth I ken it's a pernicketie situation but can't we at least get tae know each other afore we fin' another solution?"

"Very well," I agreed.

I was assigned a room in the palace and found lovely clothes to wear in the closet. I was fitted for a dress that would be my wedding gown and then I was able to spend time with Kellen. If I was the kind of girl who was swayed by fine clothes and wealth I would have married him then and there- but I was not. I wanted love and someone who loved me back.

Kellen however went out of his way to show me the beauty of the fairy world. He was nothing if not diligent in his attention to me. He showed me his people working hard to harvest the food we ate. He showed me fairies spinning materials they made into clothing. Our days were full. On the sixth day he knocked at my bedroom door at sunrise. I opened the door and as he requested.

"Hurry and get dressed Elizabeth, or may I call you Bess?"
"You can call me Bess." I responded, "What is your hurry?"
"I want to give you a day you'll never forget but to do so we have to leave in the next few minutes."

I was curious but also a little wary. Tomorrow I was expected to marry him and although I had gotten to know him better, was I ready for that step? My stomach was doing cartwheels just thinking about the ceremony they expected me to go through with. Maybe his day that I'd never forget would distract me if only for a little while?

As soon as I was dressed I stepped outside of my room, "I'm taking ye to yer foremaist surprise," Kellen claimed as he blindfolded me.

He led me through the palace and out the front doors and some distance away. I could feel the soft grass under my shoes and smell the honeysuckle in the air and knew I was in the meadow. Kellen lifted my blindfold to show me a picnic breakfast laid out before me. There were succulent grapes and honeydew melons cut in quarters.

"I am not fond o' porridge but ah ken you are so I had them make this for ye. It's sweetened with honey from oor bees," Kellen offered to me holding out a bowl that had been covered to keep it hot.

I was flattered he cared enough to find out what I liked for breakfast. I knew he liked berries and cream with a touch of honey. We sat eating on the grass, a blanket spread out with foods and fairy mead in wine glasses. A deer appeared at the side of the forest.

"That is a deer trapped in neither world. He cannae enter our fairy world but he is a majestic buck is he na."
"I wish he could be set free," I retorted feeling like the buck trapped in the in between.
"Come we wull go to the fairy spring Bess," Kellen exclaimed sensing my mood change.

We walked a great distance across hill and dale until we entered another meadow. There in the distance was not a spring as I had pictured but a glorious waterfall spouting out of a cliffside. Kellen led me to the waterfall and held out a ring that he took off his finger and put it on a golden chain he pulled from his pocket. The ruby ring had a symbol in either side that I had seen on the King's throne.

"You are unhappy and you don't want to marry me. At least not yet. I know this, so I set you free. Behind this waterfall is a place where fairy and the human world meet and the veil is thin enough for you to cross. I will keep your parents safe this is my pledge. If you should decide you want to come back just call my name and put on this ring I give you freely and whisper, *'Kellen fairy prince of Scotland true. My affianced until I say I do. I call you once I call you twice. I call you thrice. To bring you to my side. For in your heart I do abide.'*

"But would that not mean I must marry you at some point," I asked.

"Bess ah wid nae force ye. If at ony time you'll waant tae be free from oor troth call me thus 'n' I wull free ye. But if you call me this way it is a bind. It makes you my bride."

I was being offered my freedom and protection for my parents. Should I take it? I felt too young to marry even if I did have affection for Kellen. I kissed him gently on his cheek and replied..., "Thank you Kellen. I realize how great a sacrifice this is. Perhaps one day I will return to marry you."

Then I stepped through the waterfall and was once again in the Scotland I knew. I recognized the waterfalls on Scotland's human side as a spring near my grandfather's home. I walked briskly to his house. When I arrived at grandfather's house I brushed the mud from my shoes and entered the house.

"Is it you granddaughter? Have ye brought back yer faither Jaime?"

"You were willing to trade me for my father, Jaime. Did you not fear for my safety?"

"Ye huv th' fairy blood. They wouldn't nae harm you. I needed mah wee jimmy back."

"And yet they cast me out," I lied angry at his deceit.

"Whit have ye dane lassie that ah shall nae see mah Jaime again?"

"Maybe it is what you have done grandfather."

"You were gone four years. Whit did ye dae tae make thaim hate ye so?"

"Four years? But I've only been gone a week."

"Na lassie 'twas four lang years bit ye come back in time tae save yer fowk. If the fairies wull nae have ye for mah Jaime then mibbie a wean from yer union with Laird MacCormack kin save him. The mairriage contract kin now be fulfilled and the dowry paid tae save oor homes. We go then tomorra tae make Laird MacCormack honor the contract signed afore ye disappeared. 'N' dinnae think aboot escaping ye wull mairie him even if ah huv tae bar yer door."

I had left Kellen and the fairyland to be bartered again like this? Out of the frying pan and into the fire. Would he believe me if I told him Jaime didn't want to come back? I truly believed he would not. I now appeared destined to be some man's bride and my child stolen for the fairies gift so my grandfather could get his Jaime back. What could I do?

I couldn't believe this. I had been locked in my room the last three days but I'm getting ahead of the tale.

After I came to my grandfather's home he told me that I was to marry Laird MacCormack. I tried to ask questions about who Laird MacCormack was.

"Whit does it matter tae ye? Ye will mairie him. Your once faither has died 'n' yer mother is penniless. Yer mother the hauf wit thinks wi' her looks tae capture a husband in London. Her looks are not whit wee she had. She's one and thirty now efter all'."

"My father is dead?"

"Aye. 'Twas th' shock o` yer disappearance. He hud an apoplexy 'n' then he died three days efter. Yer tae blame."
"I'm to blame? Who fed me to the fairies ring?"
"Ah have decided tae forgive ye, provided ye mairie Laird MacCormack."
"I will not old man, you are to blame for this predicament. You take responsibility for your actions. I will not marry someone I don't know," I insisted.

This uncharacteristic outburst from me rewarded me with a slap across my face, so hard I fell to the floor. I was jostled as my arms were seized by servants and I was hustled to my room. Locks were hammered into the other side of the door and I heard their clicks as they latched against me. My grandfather had decreed that I would stay her until I conceded to his wishes. I was grateful the servants had thought to welcome me home with fragrant fresh fruit and a pitcher of water, for that is all I had the last three days.

I heard a knock a t my door and then heard..., "Dearest? It's mother."
"Mother? Will you let me out?"
"Nay I cannot but I will come into to talk."

Mother entered and did look older than her thirty one. Her hair had streaks of silver that she had tried to cover but didn't succeed. Wrinkles now appeared beneath her eyes, so like mine and more creases beside her mouth.

"You must do your duty child and marry Laird MacCormack." my Aunt/mother commanded
"I am only fifteen and not ready for marriage besides you are my Aunt not my mother."
"I raised you I rocked you as a babe. I comforted you when you fell down and skin and your knee. I am your mother not she who did not want you whose people cast you out." mother said hurt.

I felt bad she had raised me, then I remembered the servants had rocked me and comforted me not her but then she had not been my real mother only my foster mother. But maybe she did have sliver of love for me though I feared... not. She only really cared about her needs and her wants after all. I had seen that time and time again growing up as she treated my father with disdain and cruelty when she didn't get what she wanted. Any remnant of my feelings for her then fled. She wouldn't fool me with this feigned love. I must have looked at her oddly for she continued..., "You've been gone for four years which makes you nineteen. I married at fourteen. You are not too young and your family's fortune depends on your marriage. You will do this. He will make you a good husband he is wealthy."

"Is he kind and gentle? Will he talk with me? Share his life with me? Tell me stories and make me laugh."

"You are a foolish girl, money triumphs all of that."

"You would say that."

"Have you ever wanted girl? Have you wished for something beautiful to wear and the plants not to fail? That the sheep would yield a huge crop of wool? Have you worried the bailiff would come pull you from your home for taxes to the King? I have suffered so, you have never wanted. But you will, if you don't help your family by marrying Laird MacCormack. He will be at dinner this evening and you will be a lady. You will not refuse his proposal and you will marry him on Saturday. Is that understood?"

"You can't make me."

"I can. There are other men who are not as nice. I could sell you to and get much more of a dowry. Be happy that this man will treat you well. He won't beat you and has promised a generous allowance to you. And once you bear his son and heir you may go your separate ways."

"You expect me to sell my child to this man?"

"You are a foolish child. It's time to grow up. You will have wealth position and your own life as long as you are discrete," my mother continued.

"All of this, if I marry a man I don't know and love. Then give him a son," I said sarcastically.

"That's correct dear now you are thinking clearly." My foster mother replied thinking I was agreeing, "I'll let you think on it until tonight. The servants will come this afternoon to make you comely for your fiancée. Think hard Elizabeth and you best do the right thing. Father can be very cruel when thwarted."

I thought about my Mother and how she had been married at fourteen. Was that the reason she was so bitter? She didn't really love my father but had been sold to him as I was now being sold to Laird MacCormack? If she hadn't escaped her marriage how could I? The windows were barred the door locked. If I could convince them I would marry him, maybe I could take refuge with Kellen? I realized while talking of marriage what I wanted. Kellen had offered me all of these things. He was kind, gentle and caring. He talked to me, listened to me, and he cared about my needs not his own. Good grief, I was in love with him. I had to see and be with him. I pulled the ring from my around my neck and chanted, *"Kellen fairy prince of Scotland true. My affianced until I say I do, I call you once I call you twice, I call you thrice. To bring you to my side. For in your heart I do abide."*

Nothing happened. Kellen didn't appear. Where was he? What had happened to him? I wondered. Could he have paid for my escape? Had his father imprisoned him or was it the elfin King?

"You cried missy?" Robin Goodfellow a short burly unlikely looking fairy stood in front of me.

"Where is Kellen?"

"He lies in jyle by yer hand."

"Jyle?"

"Aye what you call prison."

"Prison where? Who has him?"

"Ye dae nae care," Robin answered.

"I care, or I would not have tried to summon him."

"Wull ye risk yer lee tae save him frae th' elfin jyle?"

"I will."

"Then it be true looove. 'n' ne'er say Robin Goodfellow doesn't hulp th' coorse o' true looove. We wull sleep oan it 'n' in the earlie morrow we shall gang tae save him."

"I have to go to dinner with the Laird and play the simpering maiden tomorrow though we shall save Kellen."

"Wha is this Laird? Shall ah slay him fur Kellen?"

"No, I'll handle him then we shall rescue Kellen."

"Very weel then bit if he tries anythin' Robin wull be there."

It seemed I had to escape and do the rescuing. I would play nice get them to let down their guard. They would believe I was the simpering maiden, sct to marry Laird MacCormack for my family's sake. I had a prince to rescue because I believed Robin only his imprisonment would keep Kellen from coming to me.

~0~

Evening dawned and I dressed in the garment, my mother had quickly procured for me. She had had a seam stress come in and alter it so it fit me like it was made for me. It was white and delicate with lace throughout it like gossamer. A fine golden thread was woven throughout lighting it up like a ray of sunlight. The neck however was indecently low. The newest fashion hype was to bare one's bosoms. I found myself picking up a needle and thread and sewing in a panel made from a handkerchief, to hide my charms from Laird MacCormack. I felt fully justify as I must not make myself appealing in any way to Laird MacCormack. I would wear it tonight then remove it and pack it carefully to take with me. It would make a wonderful wedding dress to marry Kellen.

I waited in the drawing room escorted there by the butler and a guard of servants at the door. It was clear, I still was not trusted. If I hope to escape tonight, they must be convinced I would agree to their wishes and marry Laird MacCormack. Robin had promised to come back this evening when I called and help me escape to save Kellen but I couldn't do that with all these guards watching my every move.

The doors to the drawing room opened and Mother ushered herself in followed by a man .This man was tall over six feet but old .He had to be near fifty. He stood very erect reminding me of a military man. His hair was greying at temples, thin and sparse in places. This couldn't be Laird MacCormack? Technically I was nineteen since I had spent four years in the fairyland but I still felt fifteen. They couldn't really expect a girl of fifteen to marry someone in his mid-fifties?

Mother carried on a conversation with him.. Mother had put on a dress that made her look younger and beautiful. It matched her blue eyes perfectly. She smiled and preened. I'd never seen her so animated. She seemed enamoured with him. She should be the one to marry him I thought, then a light bulb went off in my head. I could convince them they should be together and solve everything. My mother would be happy and rich and I could feel I wasn't leaving my family in the lurch to marry Kellen.

"Elizabeth plays the harpsichord," Mother exclaimed interrupting my thoughts.
"Mother."
"Now Elizabeth, you could always play the piano. She has a lovely voice," Mother growled continuing unabated.
"We haven't met I'm Laird Bruce MacCormack." He introduced himself to me.

The thing was I liked him. He was a very kind man, but too old for me and not my beloved Kellen. He would make a great stepfather even if I never saw either of them again. He must see me as a child and my mother as the woman he should marry.

I was feeling naughty and I began to play '*I Would I Were a Fairy*' *by R.F. Houseman and Miss Augusta Browne.*

"Elizabeth that song is not appropriate. Really quit acting as a child."
 "How old are you Elizabeth? I thought you were nineteen years of age but you don't look older then fifteen."
"My mother has incredible genes she's passed on to me."
"Aye ah know. I met yer mither when she wis thirteen."
then turning to my mother he asked, "Do ye mind Ainsling? Your horse wis a gied the pitch 'n' ah stopped it?"
"Aye. I remember,the horse shimmied, I fell and you caught me."

"Do you remember the kiss Ainsling?"

"Laird MacCormack you forget yourself. You are engaged to my daughter."

"Aye but twas nae I that signed th' contracts but my Father."

"So you will not honour your word?"

"We shall see I shall surely marry a Yarbourough," He replied vaguely.

He starred straight past me seeing my mother not me. My plan was working he saw me as a child not the woman he should marry. He was thinking of marrying her. I knew it. I smiled back at him conspiratorially then I picked out a sheet of music.

"Sing '*Oh! Susanna*'. The song came out last year and its very pretty," mother encouraged taking the sheet of music I had picked and placing back on the piano below her choice.

"Not last year mother it was written way before I was born. It came out in 1848.Why that's over forty years ago."

"Oh, a song from mah youth!" Laird MacCormack commented,. "Please go ahead 'n' sing it."

I knew he was older than I thought. Maybe he was fifty-five? No, his hair was white, but I was starting to believe he was closer to mother in age perhaps only seven or eight years older than her, especially after his story. If I could only get them to dance together my plan would work.

"I shall sing and play the song, but you and mother must dance to it."

"Aye Ainsling it wid be fin tae dance tae sic a song."

"Very well then, one dance wouldn't hurt."

My mother and Laird MacCormack danced across the floor.
My mother seemed like but a girl in his arms. Delight
showed in her face. When I finished the song she looked
embarrassed and flushed and sought to gain back her
composure.

"May I have a few minutes alone with your daughter?"
asked Laird MacCormack.

My foster mother's face showed pain that she quickly hid,
as she ensconced to his request leaving the drawing room.

"Elizabeth?" began Laird MacCormack.
"I can't marry you," I finished.
"How did ye ken that wis whit ah wanted tae say?" Laird
MacCormack asked in surprise.
"It's in every look you give my mother. How long have you
loved her?"

"I fell in love with her whin bit a laddie o' nineteen 'n' she
wis thirteen, to young tae court 'n' marry. Ah waited two
years bit whin ah cam back she wis married to yer faither."
"You love her still?" I queried.
"Aye ah do. If she'll huv me wull ye be mah daughter."
"You know I'm adopted? What if she can't have nay
children?"
"If we huv na bairns mah nephew Fergus wull be mah
heir."
"Then you have my blessing Father," I exclaimed.
"Now to git mah bride and convince her she is," Laird
MacCormack pronounced.

I only hope Grandfather would be as willing of his suit. I
watched him leave then slipped up to my room collecting
everything I wanted to take with me in a small burlap bag. I
wrote out a letter to my mother and Laird MacCormack.

Love is rare and worth its weight in gold. I seek my love and will be reunited with him. If I can, I will come back to visit you someday. Until then be happy together. Love each other and make up for lost time.
Your loving daughter
Elizabeth

I summoned Robin once more with the ring and he appeared.

"Urr ye ready tae put right yer wrong 'n' save Prince Kellen?"
"I am we shall save him and then ..."
"'n' then thare wull be th' finest fairy bridle we've ever seen." Robin interrupted.
"Aye the finest fairy wedding anyone has ever seen, but first we must save my beloved Kellen. How are my parents Jaime and Eolande?"
"They ur merrit 'n' living happily in th' Elfin world. Eolande 'n' Jaime huv baith asked fur Kellen release bit th' Elfin Laird hears thaim not."
"Tell me all Robin, where is he being held?" I begged.

"Mistress th' elfin King Aelfric wis angered by yer disappearance 'n' he blamed Kellen. He teuk him foremaist tae th' elf world 'n' then he sent him tae th' Goblin King Petrus .He lies in a Goblin jyle."
"Then we will conceive a plan and save him for I am of elfin blood and fairy and I can save my beloved," I claimed, shaken but determined.

We sneak out of the house. Walking over some hills what seem like hours we reach a place I'd never been before near some falls. Robin points to behind the falls and utters...,
"Here is th' gate mistress, step o'er 'n' we shall tarry tae th' Goblin King's world."

I follow his advice stepping through and we trudge towards the Goblin village. I stop and consider a plan to save Kellen. I would succeed he would be free. He saved me I would save him.

~0~

W alking down the long dark path I began to falter.

How was I to defeat a Goblin King and get back Kellen? No I was determined whatever it took I would get Kellen back. He was only in this position because he had let me go.

"So Robin tell me anything you know about the Goblin King." I demanded
"What do you know about Goblins?"
"Nothing. I've heard of them but that's all."
"Goblin's ur thieves though they prefer tae think o' themselves as borrowers. They ur quick sae ne'er can turn yer back oan them or you'll lose yer purse. They like tae negotiate. Ah think they like the arguments. They like tae align themselves with maist powerful especially if thare is a deal in thare fur thaim. Thay lik' tae kick back a draft of the mead or twa They have a strict code if someone saves thair life they ur indebted tae that being fur life. That being becomes part o' the Goblin clan."
"So you get on their good side. We will try that Robin. Maybe give them something in trade for Kellen but what have I to give them? How can I locate him?"
"Did ye bring jewels? They like gold, silver 'n' braw stones."
"I have my pearls and my grandmother's ruby necklace she bequeathed me."
"Ah then th' rubies wull have tae do. Come noo we have miles tae go 'til we reach their encampment."

We marched for hours and when I grew tired it was then we stopped as we came into a copse that enclosed the path, I saw a lake hidden amongst the trees. The lake was bordered by two cliffs and the path I was now on.

What an idyllic place for a picnic I thought taking out my packed food and the bread and cheese I had. It was if serenity had completely overtaken me. I sat down then handed some food to Robin. Would we have to swim to the edge to climb the cliffs and continue our journey? Robin sitting next to me suddenly shouted to me, oddly enough I heard it as a whisper.

"Hide behind the tree. This is a dangerous steid."

I scampered to hide from whatever had frightened Robin. I peered out and to my surprise saw figures high on the cliff top above the lake.

Robin uttered something I just couldn't quite hear, as I saw figures fighting up on the cliff. Two massive creatures seemed to be fighting with the smaller one. They were hideous to look at with wrinkled gangly bodies, the colour of dried earth, eyes hidden in their long tangled dirt filled hair the length of their body. Their noses were pink and long hiding their mouths, and feet the size of newborn babies. They shook the other creature red in colour. It's ears pointed and erected close to its skull, It's eyes pleading with the heavens for its life were yellow. I noticed its mouth was filled with numerous spikey teeth as it pleaded with the monsters not to harm it. The monsters took the small creatures' long gangly arms tied them behind its back and then tying his feet also with rope threw him into the lake with a huge splash.

"I cannot swim," cried the figure as his head bobbed up and down in the water but they laughed and ran away.

My heart went out to the creature. This seemed cruel he was terrified of the water. Before I had even thought about it I dove in. I had been swimming in the locks since I was a child every summer at my grandfather's .I could swim better than most men. Grandfather had marvelled at it but told me to keep it to myself as some would think me a witch for my prowess.

The being struggled as if he thought I was trying to drowned him but I managed to wrestle him to shore after he passed out. I began to breathe life into his mouth, as I had seen the horse doctor breath into the newborn colt.

"Do ye ken who ye have saved?" asked Robin, shocked when he saw the face of the creature life I protected.
"I've never seen him before. It is a he right?" I asked seizing my breath sounds into him hearing his lungs fill with air.
"Aye, tis a he. He's..."
"He's glad to meet such a beauteous lassie," the creature I saved replied his yellow gold eyes now starring up at me.
"Hello I'm..."
"She's Bess. Future Queen o' th' fairies 'n' future Queen o' th' Elfin 'n' nae fur th' likes o' ye," Robin answered."
"Bess? The great legend Bess?" asked the creature before me then started reciting...,'*Fairy and queen.*
A child named Bess
We do confess
Will save the fairies
When she marries
From war and doom
When a fairy seeks a boon
She will fear and run away
But coming back another day
After calling her ring
Will save Goblin King
From nasty Trolls who seek to kill

Save of her own free will
And thus achieve immortality
As Goblin King sees the reality
Goblin kin acknowledged now
Bess shall be of tribes all three
And all shall attend her on bended knee.'

"I'm King Petrus of the Woodland Goblins." He responded speaking to me as he concluded, "Thank you for saving my life fair Bess. Now marry me."

Ugh, why was it that the first thing out of these men's mouths, even supernatural men's mouths was, 'Marry me?'

"I can't marry you. I'm already married to Prince Kellen of the Fairies.

"Nonsense, he's not married. He would have told me. He was supposed to marry an Elizabeth, but she ran away."

"I did not run away. I went home to tell my otherworld family. We are married," I insisted.

"Have you said the marriage vow before witnesses?"

"We have," I lied.

"My son shall celebrate your reunion then this night," King Petrus commanded, "And I shall give you your bridegroom, if that is what he wishes."

"Your son? No, I am married to Kellen."

"Kellen is my son. I made him so when he saved me from the gargoyles. I offered him his choice of bride, but he has not picked one."

"Is he well?" I asked ignoring this.

"Kellen is well. I must caution you though Kellen is my son and now my heir under goblin law, if he doesn't want to be your groom anymore then I will decide your fate. Now come we head to the Goblin woodlands."

We followed the path. Hidden beyond some trees I saw the path went around the lake. I would see Kellen soon and I looked forward to it but would he still want me? I cringed as Petrus looked over at me in a look akin to lust.

"She is merrit tae Kellen ye best forget her except as yer daughter," Robin pronounced sounding annoyed.
"You must still prove your marriage when we arrive and if your free then instead we will marry," Petrus suddenly stated.
"As ah said she is merrit 'n' beyond yer reach except as faither,"Robin responded putting me beside him and out of Petrus' reach."
"Kellen is my husband true. We have said the sacred fairy vow."
"We shall see," Petrus countered.

We arrived at the Goblin enclave to cheers from all the many goblins. Eyes of yellow and red starred at me. There were some red skinned ones, yellow skinned ones and forest green and they all clamoured around their King.

"Where is Kellen?" I demanded.
"Kellen went to save Petrus for the Trolls," answered one Goblin.
"Thank you Aertrius,"Petrus answered.

A huge shout rang through the air and I turned and saw Kellen. Kellen's hair gleamed as black as midnight .His hair was curly but it had grown out long and luxurious. His eyes gleaming sky blue looked at me like I was his favourite food.

"I'm not dreaming Bess, my wife and my life you are here?" Kellen exclaimed running to me.

He took me in his arms spinning me up above his head.

"So this fairy is your bride Kellen?" demanded Petrus looking dismayed.

"Bess is ma guidwife ah claim her under Marriage per verba de praesenti. She is my guidwife. We have said the fairy vows."

"And he is my husband," I declared back knowing that this was a declaration under Scots law of marriage.

"You wound me ah thought tae mak' ye mah bride. Na maiter ye wull mak' a braw daughter," Petrus exclaimed.

"You forget the prophecy," Robin claimed.

"I recited it for you all ready," Petrus whined.

"You forgot the most important part of the prophecy.""" Robin declared, "*A daughter born of fairies fair,*
A son born of elfin rare,
True love will bloom
As passions zoom
Child of passion
Not fairy, human or elfin
But all three
So shall he be
He will cross the divide
And to his love he will abide
To make a true alliance of elfin,
She'll declare she is his wife
And so together they'll make a life
As he declares her life shared
His life in her hands paired
A lasting peace for all not some
For all eternity to come.'

"I have not heard this part before. You are sure? They bring peace in their union?"

"Yes," answered Robin.

King Petrus looked over at me and then at Kellen and a slow smile came over his face that relived my worry.

"Very well who am I to argue with prophecy? You two are very clever and most suited for one another. Since I would see Kellen happy and because you both saved my life, I would see you wed before all. Robin Goodfellow can find someone to do the honours. Shall we invite all of fairyland, elfin and Goblin kin, my beloved daughter?"

"Thank you Petrus, my new father," I replied, breaking out of Kellen's grip and kissing Petrus on the cheek as Petrus blushed.

"The wedding will take a week to prepare .Your declaration must hold, so for one week you shall not see each other. This shall make your marriage day and night all the sweeter," Petrus declared, as we were pulled apart and Kellen was spirited away.

I was taken to a building nearby where I stayed for the week as around me orders were given for the wedding. A dress was carefully made for me. Silk from the finest silkworms, gold fillets and jewels were sewn into the dress by eager fairies. Gauze and lace layered over the dress to make me appear a beautiful fairy bride.

The morning of the wedding at the crack of dawn I sprang out of bed looking out of the room's windows I was appalled to find a rare rain falling down in Fairy land. Where was the wedding to take place? All the preparations had been made for an outdoor wedding.

I took a huge breath.it was early yet the wedding wasn't to take place until noon. I got up and decided to paint a picture of the wedding I envisioned.

I carefully replaced the rain with a rainbow .I pictured a cathedral grove of trees as my aisle reflecting sunlight throughout. I had painting for some time when I realized it was getting late. I put my paints aside and was helped into my dress. It was then I noticed the sun was now shining. As I was taken to the wedding I saw something that left me speechless. My painting had come alive this was where I would be married among trees of green a rainbow above us. Jaime, my father took me down the aisle decorated with garlands of flowers. My real mother sat in the front row smiling at me.

Robin had procured a priest from Scotland to preside over our wedding and when he asked who gives this woman it marriage. Four people chimed in in unison.

"Her mither 'n' ah do," Jaime stated.
"I do," the reply came from Kings, Petru, Aleferic and Fáelán.

I smiled as they shouted this but then I worried where would we live that they wouldn't fight over us?

The ceremony was soon over and the partying began. It was a magical day, but I still had fears as we danced I asked Kellen.

"They will all argue over where we will live."
"We wull travel from land tae land spending our time throughoot the lands," Kellen announced wisely to all the Kings
"For in the forest lies a land bordered on all, Elfin, Fairy, and Goblin. If you need us we will come."

Cheers erupted. They were all sure we would bring them peace. The night was soon upon us and we bid our adieus to begin our married life.

I know you think this is a fairy tale all wine and roses but no life is so and I was not a foolish girl with such silly illusions. Without strife, without argument or love lies dying. We would have our fights, our triumphs our sorrow, but the one thing we now had together was all our tomorrows'. I was content in Kellen's life and arms.

~0~

The Sword

An ancient legend tells of a sword and stone, but this was something different. It had jewels encrusted on its tang. The blade what I could see of it was topped with quillon (a circular part) and guard with a nice grip. It was made of silver and bronze quite tarnished. But I've gotten ahead of myself. I had had always wanted to visit Stonehenge and then my dream had come true, for I stood in the centre of Stonehenge. As the sun came up and shone on the stones, I felt one with the stones. The air around me whirled and I felt dizzy as the world seemed to shift. Before my eyes the stones seemed to become new again.

"The great warrior comes. See I summoned him sisters," I heard but although I heard English I knew it was in ancient dialect. Before me stood three women their hair hang long and luxurious hung down to their ankles Each had a different hair colour, one had fiery red hair ,one brown almost black and the other golden like the rays of the sun.
"He looks scrawny."
"Yes, far too skinny and no muscles," commented the other.
"I used the right spell. I know I did he will be able to remove the sword," she said pointing to a sword stuck in a huge stone.

The sword was quite spectacular as it had jewels of ruby, emerald, and diamonds encrusted on its handle and I felt the need to touch it but I held myself back.

"What is your name boy?" the brunette asked.

"Arthur," I answered.

"Good you have done well. He even has the right name Morgana." The blonde commented.

"Well boy there it is. Get on with it," said Morgana the redhead.

I put my hand on the hilt and pulled with all my might, but it wouldn't budge.

"You've failed Morgana he's the wrong Arthur. Send him back," said the brunette

"I think he's handsome, might we keep him," said the blonde touching me.

"No, you know the rules. We might borrow from time but they must all go back," Morgana proclaimed.

There was a flash of light and then I found myself on the ground in the centre of Stonehenge.

"See here you are trespassing," said a voice over my head. "And now you've knocked some of the stones down on top of you. I should arrest you but looking at the scrape on your head, I'd say you've learned your lesson. Do you want me to call an ambulance sir?"

"No, I'll be fine," I said holding my head.

I wondered if my head injury explained all of this and reached in my pocket for a handkerchief to stem the bleeding of my head. To my surprise I found ruby from the sword in my pocket .I smiled looking back at the Stones. I had had quite an adventure, but no one would believe me even with the stone but it would but me a nice life.

"Thank-you, Morgana," I said back at the stones then left less it happen again.

~0~

The Fairy Tunnel of Erin

T he fairy tunnel of Erin stretched before me. Fear struck me I had found it but the foliage seemed alive as it encompassed walls. It was a nightmare, a never ending tunnel of greenery on all sides reaching up to grab me. I ran down the logs that stretched to the light at the end hoping to avoid the greenery encompassing me too.

I ran reached the light and stepped out a beautiful garden where the sun always shone, food was plenty and life was good. I, Tuatha de Danaan, queen of the fairies, was truly home safe at last.

~0~

The Love Story of Helgi and Sváva

I had grown up knowing my destiny and yet I rebelled against it, choosing my own path. I had gone into the woods to become one with nature. This is how I had lived the last three years but the time had come and I could deny my future. I returned and my father, King Eylimi betrothed me to a great warrior, King Helgi. He took me to bed and left to fight. Word reached me that he lay dying on the battlefield and I rode my horse like the wind to his side. I begged the gods for his restoral. Odin said I had it within my grasp if I accepted my destiny. When I agreed he said, "That's much better."

I rode to Valhalla my Helgi in my arms. Odin bid me to leave him, but I would not until he told me if I brought him the warrior who had struck down Helgi. With hate in my heart I seized his life bringing him forth.

Odin tried to wiggle out of his deal but I held him to his word. Helgi and I were reborn centuries later and grew up in the same small town. Helgi whose name has changed doesn't remember me; but I remember him. He'll fall in love with me even though my name is no longer Sváva. For our love story is written in eternity, the new story of Henry and Sylvia is just a continuance of the love story of Helgi and Sváva.

~0~

There Be Dragons

In the town of Kilflyn, maidens readied for the festival of Lá Bealtaine, hoping to be chosen as May Day queen. Edana's father made her enter the contest as magic spells were spread to protect the crops the cattle and the people, as flames were burnt brightly and ashes spread throughout the village. Edana proclaimed queen, was taken to the edge of the town with only a torch. In thundering rain that came and went, the flame torch went out. Edana grew scared and wanted to go home but knew she must wait until morning.

"What's that smell?" she wondered aloud as she got a whiff of sulphur and sour eggs.
"A fair maiden is it that time again?" a voice replied, "What is your name?"
"Edana."
"Little fire, what an appropriate gift you are."
"What is your name, sir?"Edana asked trying to see him in the darkness.
"I am Roy. I am under a spell but a single kiss from a maiden fair of heart shall free me."

Edana reached out and felt a long nose and hot smelly breath close but kissed it anyway. In a moment she felt a change and Roy laughed, "It works. You are now my dragon mate forever more. We shall protect Kilflyn and keep them safe. Until the masses forget the old religion, than we shall live no more."

So if you look up into the night sky and see the outline of dragons you see Edana and Roy protecting Kilflyn.

~0~

Though Shall Not Suffer a Witch to Live

I lived in the town. Helped people provided, herbal remedies when they were ill. I thought that they liked me at least. First came the whispers, then I heard the innuendos and the lies. Then they seized me from my bed in the middle of the night calling me a witch.

I was scared as they held me in the cold and provide me with no blanket no food and little water. They came tortured me with their devices and then when I didn't provide the answers they wanted they took me to the sacred lake where a black tar covered the surface. The substance of which they blamed me. I managed to swim to shore and they condemned me again.

What can I say it was miraculous I emerged covered in tar and emaciated but barely alive. People I knew all my life had done this to me. Why you ask because I dared to be different. I cured the ill, therefore I was a witch condemned to die tarred and burnt in a pit. For three long days I struggled to be free, finally I was. I stomp down the road entering the village.
The village burnt and my heart shrivels. I have turned into what they most feared, reborn in the veil of death.

They fear me but I wish only to be left alone. I live in a cabin in the woods feared by the village enough that they leave me alone. My scars and my legend have kept suitors from me but I long for a child.

One day a child barely seven unfettered by an adult appeared knocking at my door. I do not answer but she knocks louder.

"Aunt Avice it is me Mathilda Avice George. I am your great-niece."
"You are not afraid?"
"No, I've come to live with you I have no other relative but you. I know of what the evil villagers did to you but I beg you take me in and teach me how to heal. Please," Mathilda begged.

And so I had a child to nurture ad teach my ways. The village tolerated her and did not fear her but I still feared they'd turn on her so I told them that if an evil befell Mathilda so would evil befall their town. All went well until one villager fell in love with Mathilda.

Thomas adored Mathilda and wanted to marry her; but his mother and father opposed it. So they ran away to two towns over and were married in my presence by a priest.

I let them live with me but one night the towns people came demanding that I and Mathilda take the spell off Thomas. Thomas told them he wasn't be-spelled and they went away. However in the dead of night they returned burning us alive.

In my last breath I condemned them cursing the village that had condemned myself and the young lovers to death.

For no one shall find true happiness in Allerp until true love is accepted when two lovers' families accept their love unconditionally and neighbours love each other.

So if you settle in Alerp be open to love encourage and love your neighbour as you would yourself. Break the curse once and for all.

~0~

Thank-you for reading this story; if you enjoyed this story please think about leaving a few words for me at your favourite retailer
~Sincerely S.G. Lee
Please continue reading an excerpt from A Penny Saved A Murder Earned

Excerpt from A Penny Saved A Murder
Earned- Chapter 1

Chapter 1- Bloody Shoes

"A penny saved is a penny earned" ~ Benjamin Franklin

T he blood streaked across the floor, but he had carefully sidestepped it. Stupid bitch! She got what she deserved. How dare she defile his Angel's property? He hadn't left a trace...had he? No, he was too clever by half.

"I didn't spot you entering. Working late? You have an early opening tomorrow." A voice he didn't recognize interrupted his thoughts.

"Wait a minute, you aren't the lady. Who are you? You shouldn't be here," the man continued clearly alarmed.
"You shouldn't be here either," the murderer insisted.
"You killed Megan. I'm telling."
"This was something you shouldn't be allowed to see."
"I'm leaving. I didn't notice anything," the man lied, witnessing the blood.
"I'm sorry pal. Wrong place, wrong time!" the killer answered.

The homeless man ran dodging racks, finally deciding to hide behind some shelving. The killer ran after him, puzzled for a moment because he could see no trace of the homeless person. The murderer then laughed, as he realized how foolish the vagrant was being, his stench gave him away. He subdued the man with a Taser gun. Waiting seconds he then pulled him from his hiding place. Taking ties from within his pocket; he fastened the man's arms and feet. Satisfied that the homeless person was now trussed up like a turkey, he smiled.

"Please! I don't want to die!" the man cried, visibly sweating and starting to shake.

The man tried to kick out his legs and arms but failed. "You've heard about fate? Well sorry but this is your fate, buddy!" the murderer explained.
"Please! Couldn't you let me go? I won't tell! I'll move to another city. Besides who would listen to a homeless man?"
"Someone would. My Angel would."

The homeless man then smiled as if to gain trust from this killer, "You won't hurt the lady who owns the store, will you?" he asked.
"I would never harm my Angel. How dare you?" the killer responded outraged.
"Sorry! I didn't mean to insult you! Please just let me go...."
"What is your name?"
"My name is Al."

The killer put his gloves back on and smoothed them and then turned his back on his victim.

"You're going to kill me now. Aren't you? Just don't harm the sweet lady who owns this store. Will it hurt?" the man asked resigned.

"I would never hurt my Angel. She is sweet isn't she? Unfortunately that makes unscrupulous people take advantage of her."

"I promise I would never take advantage of her kindness. She's the best part of my day and this city, Happy Valley, Ontario. She picked me up from the gutter and helped me."

"I know you wouldn't and it hurts me to do this. Tell you what though, I'll make your death painless because I like you, Al," the killer offered, feeling suddenly sorry for the man. Then he checked himself.

Living on the streets was hell; maybe he was doing the guy a favour? Yes, of course he was. Taking a pill bottle out of his pocket and opening the dispenser, he placed some in a coffee cup he took from the sideboard. Then he filled the cup with the tepid coffee from the coffee pot, stirring the pills in rapidly.

"Please couldn't you let me go? I won't tell and I'll watch over her when you're not here."

"Sorry, times up, Al. Here now, drink this coffee," the assassin commanded placing the mug at Al's lips.

Al tried not to drink and spit some of the coffee out, but the assassin plugged his nose and the cup was soon empty.

"Admit it Al, you had a crappy life. Just give in and go to the light. I hear good things wait there for people like you," the killer stated.

Al tried to fight some more, but he soon found it was losing battle. Al's breathing slowed as he slipped into a deep sleep and stopped breathing altogether. His age and living on the streets made the pills work fast.

Now what to do with the body? The killer thought. His Angel must not find this man here, bad enough he left Megan's body here for his Angel to find. This man knew his Angel; she cared, so like her to look after the homeless. The dumpster of course! The day after tomorrow was garbage day. Covered in garbage no one would find Al.

~0~

The next day
Lily

Ominous clouds replaced the morning's sunlight
turning the skies to shades of deep purple and navy blue, streaked with gray. Lily Kelly stared at the sky for moment, and then departed the courthouse doors in Happy Valley, Ontario, Canada, skipping down the steps. The city looked it's age of over a hundred as the buildings downtown looked old and decrepit. If only the town could find some money to fix downtown Lily thought. Like most small towns the tax monies were drying up as the tax base moved on and out.

Lily's mind turned to Amelia, her cousin and best friend. Amelia needed Lily to support her in her grief. She had a fight with her husband Horace again this morning about how much time he was spending at the office. Lily was always working, and so was Horace, so how much time was Rose their fifteen year old daughter getting? She had won in court, but all she could think about was her family. Everyone needed her and she felt like she was being pulled in three different directions. Something had to give and it looked like it was her job. She would have to cut back on some of her work. Her family had to come first.

Lily stumbled some more over the steps only stopping from hurrying across the courtyard to her office, when her heel broke on her shoe. Today was supposed to be about her victory after her win in court; but it appeared with her expensive shoe's heel breaking, she was mistaken. They ought to get the ruts in the paving stones fixed; that was her reflection as she cursed her bad break. What did they say about omens? Maybe she should have taken a hint from the heavens' darkening? She noted as her bad luck had seemed to get worse with the arrival of some reporters.

"Ms. Kelly, give us a statement about the Rockwood case?" yelled one reporter.
"Ms. Kelly, how does the Sulimani family feel about your victory?" yelled another.

One bold reporter stepped forward, "Crown Attorney Kelly, congratulations on your win. Was it hard to try a case which involved a council member?" asked Paul Knight from the local television station, thrusting a microphone in Lily's face.

"Anyone who commits a crime in Happy Valley will be tried by the Crown with the full force of the law, despite their office. So no, I did not find it difficult to do my job," Lily replied testily.
"Thank-you, Ms. Kelly. What does the Sulimani family think about the judgement?"
"Amani Sulimani was five years old, when Zebadiah Rockwood's truck went through a red light. His truck struck the back of the Sulimani's SUV killing her. He then left the scene pursued by good Samaritans, who wished to stop Mr. Rockwood from continuing driving drunk: a pursuit caused by Mr. Rockwood's actions, which put a number of lives in danger."

"Will the family be comforted with this conviction?" queried another reporter.

"Amani Sulimani existed as their only child. Mr. Rockwood's conviction will not bring her back, but hopefully will bring some peace of mind to her family knowing he will be behind bars." Lily answered.

"Do you sense, given your own personal tragedies that you'll be able to get a sentence fitting the crime?"

"My family's history does not come into my trial cases, only the person's guilt."

"And when will sentencing take place?" asked another reporter.

"Sentencing will take place next month."

"Thank-you Ms. Kelly. This is Paul Knight reporting, with an update on the Zebadiah Rockwood's drunken driving case. Zebadiah Rockwood was a long time council member here in Happy Valley. He took a leave of absence to deal with his legal issues. Mr. Rockwood was charged with impaired driving causing death, two counts of failing to remain at the scene of an accident and dangerous driving last December. When asked about the conviction today Mr. Rockwood and his lawyer issued a no comment but indicated they will release a press release tomorrow. We will have the complete story for you at six pm. Paul Knight reporting for CHPV-TV."

Lily hated speaking on camera, even though it was part of her job as the Crown attorney, so she was glad the scrum had been completed. She hated sounding tough and unyielding but it was all in the description of her job title. She had fought difficult challenges to get this job and she had to work hard and fight hard to keep it. After all there were aspects of her job her she loved like putting the bad people that would harm others away. The press was gone and she was now free to go to her office to file her reports and leave early. She crossed the street, entered her building and went straight up to her office.

"Victory is mine!" Lily Kelly cried triumphantly as she walked into her office.

"So you won?" asked Colleen Finn, her administrative assistant.

"I did and I bested Michael Taylor. He thought he would beat me in court. He actually believed his client would win."

"Good for you, boss, I knew you would nail his lily white ass to the wall. He's such a scumbag lawyer all his clients seem to be as guilty as hell."

"Colleen! Language! But yes, I did," Lily answered, showing pearly white teeth and laughing to take the sting out of the reprimand.

Colleen looked expectantly at Lily and she felt stupid did she miss something? Oh the joke! Lily hadn't laughed at Colleen's wit.

"Funny, I got it. Zebadiah Rockwood's sentencing takes place next month, but he will be held until then; no bail, no goodbyes to his favourite water hole. As the Crown, I'll recommend the longest sentence I can get. It's victories like these which make my job worthwhile. I don't know how much satisfaction this will give that little girl's family, but at least they'll know her killer remains in jail. He can't take another life again, because he will be incarcerated."

Lily went over to her desk and sat down.

"Can you imagine Michael Taylor, tried to use the defence that Rockwood was not drunk. Just tired? He claimed Rockwood drank only after the accident, while driving his company's truck; so the company couldn't possibly be responsible"

"I can believe it!" Colleen agreed, "I'm glad you proved he'd drank so much before getting in the truck. That proved he was legally under the influence when the accident occurred. I hope I was some help in that aspect."
"Of course were."
"Thanks, Lily."
"It's still early; only nine forty-five, and my day's clear until what, two-thirty?"
"That's correct." Colleen replied.

Colleen checked a day planner, frowning.

"Is everything okay? You seem a little down."
"Everything is fine. Amelia's grand opening starts at noon, but I promised to be there sooner if possible. If I go right now, I'll surprise her," Lily grabbed her coat to leave.
"After what happened to her, Amelia needs the encouragement."

"Amelia does need support and she'll always have it in me. Hold all my calls Colleen. Unless it's urgent then call my cell."
"I'll do that. Tell Amelia, I hope her store has great success. What time should I say you'll be back?" Colleen responded to a departing Lily.
"Tell whoever asks that I'll be back after two p.m..."
"And if they ask where you are?" Colleen questioned.
"Tell them I'm meeting with a witness," Lily replied with a wink.
"If there's cake bring me back a piece. Please, boss?" Colleen begged.
"I ordered a cake, but it's not supposed to arrive until one thirty so we'll see. I'm leaving now. Remember only urgent calls to my cell phone." Lily cautioned, leaving through the front door.

She twisted her shimmering brown hair back up into its traditional bun. Pulling out her cell phone, she dialled Amelia's store. There was no answer.

~0~

A few minutes ago

A lone male walked into the store. His left hand held a gun while his right hand steadied it. He strode in with caution. His dark brown eyes dart from corner to corner, searching for an assailant. His well over six-foot tall frame slouches. He is ruggedly handsome, with dark brown hair clipped short to his head. He is dressed in a dark blue jacket and dress pants; and a badge is clipped to his belt buckle. Finding the scene secure he putting his gun away and pulled a pair of gloves out of his suit coat pocket and a pair of booties, which he slipped on his shoes.

He checked the victim. No pulse. Advancing forward, he bent down to check the second woman; her phone still in her hand, her head bloody. He noted the second victim is still breathing, though unconscious. He looked around, as if waiting for someone. Deciding they weren't coming yet, he took out a mini recorder. He started scanning the scene and speaking aloud.

"This is Sergeant Detective Emmett Rogers. I am at the scene of a homicide, at Quirks, one forty five Maple Street. A woman lays sprawled out across the floor. The woman's arms are positioned underneath her, as if to break her fall." "The back of her head and her long blonde hair are streaked in rusty-brown blood, as well as her clothing below the hair. Blood pools across the floor spiralling out in two long streams. Footprints are noticeable, as if someone stepped through the drying blood. The weapon appears to be a pair of scissors, found beneath the victim."

The man continued to speak aloud as he walked around, carefully avoiding contaminating the evidence, by stepping over a paper cup.

"A coffee cup... possibly one of those lattes is overturned. Its contents are also spilled on the floor and countertop. Coffee is spilled at the front door and possibly on the shoes. The second victim's shoes are not on the bruised victim, but on the floor. The shoes can be found near an overturned ladder, at the front door. It appears the one woman, may have been carrying a ladder and toy stock to place on the shelves, when she slipped in the blood.
The man paused to think.

"This might be a setup by the second victim to cover the actual crime. The woman, however, seemed to have the victim's blood all over her clothes and hands like she crawled through the blood. I believe there are two possible scenarios here. One the owner of the shop, one Amelia Kelly, murdered her employee and set this up to appear a perpetrator broke in and killed her accidentally hurting herself in the process. Or two... it is at it seemed that she stumbled on the crime scene."

"Is it a robbery gone wrong? It is too soon to tell. The store owner will be enroute to hospital as soon as the EMTs have arrived... interview to follow. The time is now ten twenty a.m.," he concluded turning off his recorder. He pulled out a notebook and examined the room some more taking notes.

Now
Lily and Detective Emmett Rogers

The man's eyes turned and his vision focused completely as a woman entered the store. His vision took in her tall and slender form and her long shimmering brown hair, pulled into a tight roll. He noted she was closely followed by the Emergency technicians and gave a sigh of relief. The woman entering the store had brilliant blue eyes. He had a feeling she often turned heads, even dressed as she was, in her business attire. But he noted something about the way she walked screamed money and upper class and it gave him a stir. Money always spelled trouble in his mind.

"Oh no, Amelia!" she screamed and tried to rush to Amelia, but was stopped by the man's arm.

"This is a crime scene Ma'am. We don't want you disrupting the evidence. Let the EMTs and detectives do their job. Then you can go to ...you're er...friend?" Sergeant Detective Rogers commanded.
"Crime scene? What has happened?" Lily asked politely, wanting to be cooperative.
"Ma'am, I'll know better after I assess the scene. Until then, please remain near the front door and don't contaminate my crime scene." ordered Detective Rogers briskly.
"I promise I'll stay out of the way; but at least can I get her Adrienne Changs?"
"What or who, are Adrienne Changs?" said Detective Rogers looking totally perplexed.
"Shoes, those shoes right there!" Lily pointed to a pair of heels lying behind the yellow tape.

"You're worried about shoes? Women! Do you have any idea of what's going on here?" Detective Rogers snapped, shaking his head.

"You sexist pig!" countered Lily under her breath.

"Men!" Losing her temper now and louder she continued "Those shoes are worth five hundred dollars! And she probably wore them for what a half an hour? And you want me to walk away and leave them to be destroyed!"

"Five hundred dollars for shoes? Is she crazy?" Detective Rogers asked dumfounded.

"No! She's not crazy. How dare you?" Lily asked suddenly outraged.

He was smug wasn't he? Handsome yes, but oh so smug, she questioned herself. That wasn't important. Amelia is injured on the floor and he questioned her? Instead of letting her go to her cousin! Why was she so worried about the shoes? They were only shoes. Amelia was injured; who cared about footwear?

"Sorry... the shoes are evidence. Name? Occupation? Address?" Detective Rogers barked, ignoring her statement.

"I want to see your identification first, and then you'll get the information," insisted Lily.

"I am Sergeant Detective Emmett Rogers," the man revealed, showing his police badge.

"Oh that's funny," Lily uttered laughing. "If you and Amelia were introduced it would be Aem and Em."

Lily followed this up by hysterically followed by crying. What was wrong with her? She never lost it like this. She always appeared a professional. She had seen crime scenes. She could handle this. Couldn't she? Amelia would be okay. Wouldn't she?!

"Get a hold of yourself Lily. You have embarrassed yourself." Lily heard a voice in her head, she recognized as her father's. Odd how her Dad's voice, came back to her now, she rarely saw him, since he lived in Prague and he only called about twice a year.

"Ma'am, what you are saying is not that funny. Are you all right? Maybe we should have the EMT's check you out for shock. I think your friend's okay. She might have a head injury and possibly a broken leg, but she'll be okay." Sergeant Detective Rogers then turned to the Emergency technicians (EMTs) to seek confirmation demanded "Right?"
"Should be. But head injuries can be serious. The lady seems a little shocky but not overly so. Maybe a cup of coffee or tea would be in order, " the one EMT replied.

Sergeant Detective Rogers shot him a disapproving look. "The Sergeant Detective is right. She'll be fine. She'll be taken to the hospital for treatment," the Emergency Technician agreed.
"See...what did I tell you? Now I need to see some identification and then get some answers to my questions. Name? Address? Occupation? Why are you here?" Detective Rogers barked at Lily.
"Amelia's my best friend and more. This should have been the greatest day of her life, her opening of her new store; a one of kind toy and collectibles retailer. A grand opening and now it's ruined. Who did this to her?" Lily asked, uncharacteristically wringing her hands and still trying to regain her calm, as thoughts of Amelia's demise threatened to enter her mind.
"Ma'am... she slipped in blood. She hit her head on the floor and on the ladder. No one harmed her. She did this to herself," explained Sergeant Detective Rogers.
"I realize she's clumsy, but she didn't put blood there to trip in," defended Lily angrily.

"No the blood was spilled by whoever killed the woman behind the counter."

"Someone is dead behind the counter?" Lily responded shocked and surprised.

"No comment; as I explained Ma'am this is an active crime scene. What is your name?" Detective Rogers insisted forcefully again.

"Lily Kelly-Brooksfield. My husband is Horace Brooksfield, the mayor. We live down the street on Beaconfield. Do you want the number? It's nine hundred and sixty-two." she replied condescendingly.

"If you're Mayor Brooksfield's wife… then you're the Crown Attorney." Coming to this realization, Sergeant Detective Rogers hid a sigh.

"Please update me on this active crime scene, now," commanded Lily pulling back her shoulders.

Emmett Rogers put on his professional face and smiled.

Lily just felt so angry. This cop who grinned back at her was the biggest reason. She was a married woman. She shouldn't be attracted to a cop who apparently existed to give her grief and solve a murder. She threw back her shoulders again. It was okay to look at someone attractive, she excused herself. Everyone looks, and most of the time it meant nothing. It's only if you acted on any attraction it became wrong. She would never act on the temptation. Besides he appeared to be the most annoying man she'd ever met.

"Ma'am, you know I can't fill you in on any of this case. You'll have to recuse yourself from this case, as you're familiar with the crime scene." Detective Rogers emphasized, once again interrupting Lily's thoughts.

"Why don't you just come out and say what you think. You consider me a suspect," Lily uttered.

"A lot of people are suspects in my book. I have to make a case for them committing the crime or I have to eliminate them as suspects. And don't attempt to solve this yourself; amateurs just get in the way." Detective Rogers explained, his eyes wandering.

Lily was slightly amused. Detective Rogers thought she wanted to insinuate herself into this murder investigation? She might not have before that comment, but she did now. He seemed to be focusing on Amelia or Lily as his prime suspect. Lily knew neither of them had committed this murder, so that meant she had no choice but to find out for herself who had committed this crime. She would pretend she wanted nothing to do with this situation, even as far as passing it off to her underling Barbara. After all she could always investigate behind the scenes.

Spotting the emergency technician's righting their gurney with Amelia on it, Detective Rogers exclaimed, "Oh good, the ambulance can take the victim to the hospital. Now can we can get down to brass tacks; you can fill me in on these people and anything else you know or have held back from me."

"I want to go with her," Lily protested.

Lily pulled herself back taking several steps back putting distance between herself and this cop. It was odd, how alive she felt when she jousted with him. He was a cop investigating a murder and she was married.

"Stop this now Lily!" She told herself.

"Ma'am, I realize you want to go see your friend. Before I could release you from the scene, I need something from you. We need you to identify the other victim. Maybe you'll recognize her when I turn over the body." Detective Rogers explained, softening a little, as he slipped on another pair of gloves.

"Only if you'll stop calling me Ma'am. Call me Lily or Crown Attorney Kelly but not Ma'am. It makes me feel eighty years old."

"If it will get you to identify the victim...thank-you Crown Attorney Kelly." "Let's look, shall we?" Lily agreed.

Lily took a breath as she gathered herself to observe who lay there dead. She gasped as she stared over the counter to see the back of the woman's head. She covered her mouth in horror.

"Good grief! I never realized they appear so alike from the back," replied Lily shocked.

"Who do you think she looks like Ma'am?" demanded Detective Rogers.

"What did I say about Ma'am? Don't they give you sensitivity training at Police College? You want to know who this is? This is Megan, Megan Fowler. She's an employee of Amelia's. But she works evenings she's...is....was a college student. I can't believe this is Megan. Megan is such a sweet girl and worked part-time to be able to go to school and support her mother. Why would someone kill her? Do you think it's possible someone mistook her for Amelia?" Lily rambled, tears slipping from her eyes.

"That's a possibility, Ma'am. We will explore all aspects."

"I know the drill, Sergeant Detective Rogers." Lily gave the detective a mock salute, "Why can't you admit that they mistook Megan for Amelia?"

"We don't have any of the facts yet, Ms. Kelly," replied Detective Rogers.

"What about Amelia? Is she in any danger?" asked Lily. "If I were to speculate, I suppose that could be a possibility," Detective Rogers answered non-committally.

They both watched as the technicians gathered the evidence and blood samples and took pictures before the body was taken away.

"Will someone be assigned to guard her and keep her safe?" Lily asked getting exasperated.
"That's in motion, Crown Attorney Kelly," Detective Rogers explained, trying not to sound annoyed that she's telling him how to do his job.

Detective Rogers and Lily turned as another cop swaggered into the store. Burly and well over six feet tall, his hair was dark like Detective Rogers. Unlike Detective Rogers, this man preened like a peacock; Lily was aware of the type. Guys like him smiled with their mouths and not their eyes. They thought all women should admire them and only them. She noted his smile went as far as his lips.

"What have you got here, Emmett?"
"Nothing you need to be concerned about, Brad," Detective Rogers replied, obvious tension showing between the two. "You should be able to get some great publicity out of this one," Brad said loudly to Detective Rogers.

Brad then strutted over to the murder scene.

"It's my case, Brad," Detective Rogers insisted.
"I'm not trying to interfere," Brad persisted walking around, "I just thought if you needed some help I would lend a hand. It doesn't look like something you could handle on your own."

"I don't need help, thanks, Brad. I don't need you messing up my crime scene." Detective Rogers declared "I've got it all under control.

"It doesn't look that way to me. I would solve this case quickly. You could use me in your corner," Brad continued. "We don't need you. Now the Crown Attorney is here, so I have it all in hand. Goodbye, Brad." Detective Rogers practically spat.

"Ah, the lovely Crown attorney Kelly is here," Brad exclaimed trying to sound charming but failing miserably. "And you are?" asked Lily putting her full aristocratic chill in to her voice. "I'm Brad Owens, at your service, Attorney Kelly. Sergeant Detective Brad Owens. I use to be Emmett's partner," Brad explained smiling and pointing to Detective Rogers.

Detective Rogers rolled his eyes. "Thank God you're not anymore," He stated under his breath loud enough for only he and Lily to hear.

"So what do you think, Crown Attorney? Was it a robbery gone wrong?" asked Brad.

"I'm not sure. Why do I bother to tell you this? This isn't your case," Lily commented suddenly not willing to share with Brad.

She didn't know why but something about his smile, and the way Emmett Rogers had reacted to him made her dislike him. Brad's smile was phony, like a used car salesman. It was slick and slimy. That wasn't fair to used car sales people. Lily was sure they were more honest than this phoney, Brad Owens. Lily had come across a lot of people in her job. She certainly felt she was a good judge of character. In fact, she could spot a phoney a mile away. Detective Emmett Rogers, unlike Brad Owens, appeared like he knew his job. She'd heard of him many times, but had never run into him on the job until today. Thank goodness for the Internet on her phone. He was a dedicated cop. He had done his time and had come up through the ranks, strictly on merit. Detective Rogers didn't seem to like Brad Owens and that was reason enough for Lily not to trust him.

Emmett Rogers had an exemplary record as a police officer; she trusted his instincts and knowledge over this smarmy, Detective Brad Owens. He'd get to the bottom of this. Lily wished he would let her leave soon and check on Amelia. They had spent their teen years together and were as close as sisters. She'd always felt responsible for Amelia, being two years older. She wanted to make sure Amelia was okay.

"Okay. Well if you don't need my help, I'm leaving because I have work to do. There are other crimes to investigate." Brad answered leaving, "See you around Emmett."
"Not if I see you first," muttered Emmett under his breath.
"So am I free to go?" Lily demanded.

Emmett then offered her his pen.

"I have your address, so as long as you sign here in my notebook. "You are free to go," he said gesturing.

Lily glanced over at Detective Owens and watched him leave before reaching for the book. She then signed her signature with a flourish. Detective Rogers scanned the signature, thinking momentarily it was just as elegant as Lily. He shook his head, reminding himself to stay connected to reality.

"So I am free to go, Detective?" Lily repeated.
"I said so didn't I? I'll be checking in on your friend, of course, and I may need to follow-up with you later, but as of now, you are free to go." he smiled to take out the chill in his voice but, already he felt exhausted.
"I would expect nothing else from you, Detective Rogers."

As she got into her car, Lily breathed a sigh of relief she had finally been able to leave the store.
She buckled up her seatbelt and put her car in gear. Backing the car up, Lily pulled out into the street and narrowly missed getting hit by a car, she didn't view. Luckily the other driver slammed on his brakes

She noticed the male driver shouting, "Stupid woman driver" as she read his lips in her rear view mirror. He was justified in his anger. It had been her fault, but she didn't have time to dwell.

She headed down the road toward the hospital; despite her resolve her mind wandered. She thought about poor Megan's mother getting the news of her daughter's death. It would kill Lily to get news like that about her adopted daughter, Rose. What kind of monster kills a young woman? Why did, whomever it was, have to kill Megan? It wasn't a robbery, she'd read in Detective Rogers' notes, when he gave his notebook to her to sign her statement. As Lily drove, more questions flooded into her head. Was Amelia the real target? Megan certainly appeared like Amelia from the back.

Amelia didn't appear too hurt. Maybe she suffered a concussion? Concussions could be serious; she knew from her readings. The EMT hadn't said Amelia was in serious condition though. Not that the EMT could explain before Emmett Rogers got on his case. Revving the engine, she waited impatiently for the light to go green. Once Lily reached the hospital, she could reassure herself, Amelia was all right.

~0~

Please find this book in e-book and in paperback at Amazon. Please continue reading for an excerpt from Dreams Can Kill.

Excerpt from Dreams Can Kill-Chapter 1&
2

Chapter 1-Survival

T he rain pelted down on me, as I struggled to come to
my senses. My head felt like it had split in two, as if little
lumberjacks had taken up residence. I opened one eye. The
world spun sideways like a ride at the fair. I tried shutting
one eye, then the other. I nearly fell back to sleep. I opened
my eyes again, fighting the sleep which wanted to overtake
me. I shuttered my eyes again, as my stomach protested.
My whole body manipulated, bruised, bent and broken like
some old rag doll discarded.

Sleep...sleep would solve my problems, my brain protested.
No! I had a reason I needed to stay awake and alert...A little
sleep, a part of me protested again. No, I must stay
conscious. But I remained so tired. I dragged myself across
the pebbled ground. My right leg stuck out at an impossible
angle, obviously broken. I saw by lifting my head slightly
and turning it that there appeared to be a road up ahead. I
had to get to the road. If I dragged myself that far, surely I
would be rescued?

But it was oh so hard, to drag yourself backwards, when you couldn't perceive where you were going. Oh no, what if he came back. He would finish me off...finish what he had started.

He who? Who was this person, who left me to die? Why couldn't I remember? Don't panic... the thing to do is right now is to reach help; then and only then would I be safe. I caressed large pieces of gravel which cut into the back of my head. I sensed I was close to the road. I reached out with my good hand and touched a paved surface. I knew I didn't have much strength left. I experienced the energy drain quickly leaving my body. I tried to fight the drain, but the world faded to black.

~0~

Excerpt from Dreams Can Kill

Chapter 2 - Time flies when you' re having fun

I opened my eyes slowly. A tube appeared to have been inserted in my arm, feeding me intravenously, another tube down my throat as well. The lumberjacks in my head had been replaced by a dull achy sensation, as if I wasn't quite there. I suffered from weakness all over, but my body didn't have the same sensation, as when I had blacked out on the road. My leg felt whole again and yet my leg didn't appear to be in a cast, or slung up on a tripod. How much time had passed? This definitely looked like a hospital room. The walls were pale white and I lay in a single bed. I rested in a private room how about that?

A nurse in a white cap entered the room. She grabbed my wrist and she proceeded to take my pulse. Alarmed, she stared straight into my face, "Well! Look who is awake. Welcome back to the real world," she proclaimed.

I tried to speak and realized the tube in my throat prevented that. Why was a tube in my throat I wondered? How long I been here? I assumed I looked scared because the nurse explained in a soft voice, "There, there honey, you take deep breaths, easy now."

"Why don't I go get the doctor? He can come and have a look at you and remove the tube from your throat."

I tried to nod my head in agreement but my head moved like lead. It seemed like eons before a man in a white doctor's coat appeared at my bedside. He appeared tall and lanky; with dark curly brown hair and warm deep blue eyes. Without any preamble he announced, "We will now remove this tube. Take a big breath now."

The tube came out as I gagged. Now I could ask the questions which plagued me.

"How did I get here? And where am I?" I tried to ask, croaking out the words, as if my voice hadn't been used in a while.

"Speak slowly. Here, have sips of water," answered the doctor.

"How did I get here?" I repeated, sure that I had been speaking clearer because I had taken a sip of water.

"I don't know who found you, but an ambulance brought you here in critical condition. You had a broken leg, some broken ribs, and a fractured skull."

"I came here in critical condition? So I've been here awhile?" I asked shocked.

"Yes, you've been here awhile. You were at a different hospital first. You are in Andrews' clinic now."
"Your condition appeared to be perilous there for some time. They lost you twice. We had placed you in a coma to let your brain swelling go away. Then we didn't know if you would ever come out of the coma."

He continued to explain like he couldn't quite find the words. But why would a doctor have trouble explaining a medical condition?

"I guess time flies when you have fun," I stated flippantly, hiding fear I didn't quite understand and becoming puzzled.

Why did he say first they then we? Hadn't he been there?

"I would like to examine you to see how you're doing now and get an update on your condition."

"I'm good. As you can see," I answered in response.
"I don't know if you even realize, but your speech isn't as clear as you think. You're slurring your words," he stated.
"I'm sure the words will come easier in time, but I'd like to check your reaction time and some other physical reactions."

What could he be talking about? I wasn't slurring my words. Was I?

The doctor began his examination. A flashlight flashed deep into my eyes. I blinked in response, as the light, so bright, made my eyes hurt. His response seemed to be to write down something on the chart, and pick up my wrist to take my pulse and blood pressure. He then listened to my chest with his stethoscope.

I moved my head and tried to sit up, but the effort zapped all my remaining strength. I surprised myself at how I felt like a newborn baby. He continued his examination. I grew tired but fought the sensation. If I closed my eyes for a moment, would the feeling would go away? I closed my eyelids and fell fast asleep.

~0~

I ran over hills. The night appeared so dark, and ink black; I could barely view two feet in front of me. My feet stumbled, as I tried to see the uneven ground in front of me. My palms clenched with sweat, as my heart pounded like the organ would jump out of my chest. I turned around, my eyes darting from side to side searching for my pursuer. No sign, but I knew he wasn't far behind.

My hair in a high ponytail, whipped at my face, as I picked up the pace in my flight. He seemed close enough, that I had the sensation of his breath on my neck… so close he might reach out and touch me. I turned again to see if I could glimpse him near, and I saw a man. But what puzzled me was what materialized in the man's face. Where his face should be, a gaping black hole yawned.

How could this be? The thought plagued me only for moment, as fear gripped me and survival instinct kicked in. Realizing if he caught me I would be killed, I ran stumbling over rock and uneven ground. When the inevitable happened, I tripped falling to my knees. He had me. There was no escape from my fate. I would die now. I struggled as he grabbed my left wrist twisting my arm.

This appeared no dream, I might awake from; he had me now and he would kill me.

I twisted slightly trying to free my wrist but he grabbed my other wrist and shook me slightly saying…, "Quite a dream you were having, but a dream none the less. Nothing can harm you now."

I stared into his face and slowly his look changed, from the faceless man, to another face entirely. This wasn't the man in my visions; the demon in my nightmare. I knew in my heart this remained an altogether different kind of man

This face with smiling blue eyes radiated warmth, and kindness. His face stayed gentle, not violent. I had been dreaming and had mistaken his touch for the man in my dreams. I flushed with embarrassment.

"You are quite awake now? I won't harm you. Now, do remember me?"

I stared at him, slowly waking up, and realizing where I was.

"I'm your Doctor, Doctor Andrews, at your service, my lady. We met before when you awoke from your coma," he continued speaking softly, and gently, bowing at the waist and smiling.

Shouldn't I have recognized him immediately? Heat rushed to my cheeks, as I turned red in embarrassment.

I was a fish out of water. I didn't like the way I reacted; like something had happened and all was a secret to me. I liked to be in charge of my life every aspect, and right now it seemed like I appeared in charge of nothing.

"How long have I been here?" I whispered, trying to speak louder.

"I would have said it's a lot longer, than you think," he replied cryptically.

"Do you always answer a question with a question? I want an answer for my query," I demanded angrily.

"What do you remember?"

"I believe I asked you to stop making this an interrogation. If you must know, I remember waking up a little while ago the nurse came in and then you came a little later," I answered exasperated, wondering what could be wrong with me. I didn't get angry so easily. Did I? Why did I behave this way? Everything he said seemed to make me angry.

"Your little while ago was two days ago...," he explained, breaking off as if afraid to say more.

"But that's impossible..."
"You fell into a restorative sleep. It is not uncommon for patients who have been in a coma to do so."

"Two days? I slept for two days?" I commented incredulously.

"Yes," Doctor. Andrews stated.

"How long was I in a coma?" I asked worried to hear what he might say.

"What month do you remember?"

"You have to be in charge, don't you? Questions! Questions!" I replied, delaying the answer. I was suddenly afraid that I'd been in this coma far longer than I realized, and grew angrier.

"I know you're scared. Are you sure you want to know? The information can wait," he insisted.

"I'm not scared," I lied with false bravado, "I remember quite clearly the month is March."

"It is the eleventh of September nineteen hundred and seventy-one. Do you remember what happened the day of the accident?" he asked.

"That's not possible. I can't have been in a coma for six months. Why do you lie to me?" I spat at him.

"I know it's hard to assimilate but time has passed and it is September," he insisted softly, but firmly.

"Why do you persist in a lie? What do you have to gain with this preposterous story?" I demanded; still not ready to believe this.

"Exactly! What do I have to gain? Sharron, I'm not lying to you," he stated sadly.

Until that moment I hadn't given any thought to my name, but as Doctor Andrews called me Sharron, I realized I wasn't even sure if that was my name. I didn't have a clue what my name was. My name might be Sharron, but I didn't recall the name. My name could be Mary, or Angela, or any other name in the world. If I had a surname, I couldn't remember it either. A huge blank spot stood where any recollection should be.

How could my last memory be of March, but I still had no recollection of my name, er names? This was normal after a long coma. I decided.

Perhaps my memory had been so underused, and only had temporary gaps? Or I was hungry? Yes, it had to be one of those things. A temporary aberration of the mind... No need for me to worry. No, need to share any such information.

My memory was only hiatus. That had to be the answer. Give it a few days and my memory would all come back. There was no need to tell the doctor, especially since my recollections would all come back. Absolutely not, I reasoned.

After all what good would it do to tell him? He'd look at me either with sympathy, or call in a shrink. I wanted none of the sympathy, and whispered glances which would follow. So I had a few memory gaps, nothing to worry about. It was perfectly normal after a coma, I reassured myself.

"What will you do with all this information Sharron?" asked Doctor Andrews suddenly concerned.

"I must admit the information was a bit of a shock to find the month was September and not March, but I'm over the surprise. "I'm hungry what does it take to get food around here?'' I demanded, quickly changing the subject. Besides I was ravenous.

"I think you can start some light foods, some soft foods, Jell-O soup etc.," Doctor Andrews spouted. Turning to the nurse he commanded, "Nurse get a light meal for my patient."

"Certainly Doctor," the nurse replied, coming into the room rather quickly, at his summons.
Just when I thought I had successfully gotten rid of the doctor, he turned around and said... "I know you are rather tired and hungry right now, but I'm sure you to want to discuss these revelations later today."

How could I get him to change his track? I didn't want to discuss my memory loss with anyone. I wasn't ready for anyone to find out I didn't know who I was. If I told him, would he treat me like a mental patient?

No, I wasn't going to tell him, or anyone. I needed to fake what I remembered. They'd never know, I couldn't remember. I would then have the time to accept this myself, and hopefully everything would come back. No one would ever have to know.

Wait a minute, did he know that I didn't remember? He talked about the fact I'd been in a coma, but had he given me any knowing glances? I gave him a sideways glance. Deciding he didn't have a clue about my memory problem. I plotted to keep it that way.

"There is not a lot to talk about; but if you want to we can discuss my medical condition we can get to that later," I replied, hoping he would take my response as an agreement and leave.

Luckily for me he took the hint. Maybe he would even forget to come back and discuss this later? No, I hoped for too much, but he did look convinced that I'd talk to him later. Good then he'd go away.

"I will return later, Sharron."

He then left taking his questions with him. I breathed a sigh of relief. Now alone with my thoughts, surely I'd conjure up a memory or two. First I would eat and refuel. That would help the memories, as well as my stomach.

I stared at the food the nurse had brought in. I'm starving to death and the nurse gave me not enough food to feed a rabbit? I tried to pick up the spoon and found my hand wouldn't cooperate.

"Would you like some help?" the nurse asked kindly.
"I can do it myself," I responded stubbornly.

Although I had found it difficult to raise my hand to my mouth, that soon became easier. I found by clamping my hand around the spoon I could manage to feed myself. It was then I realized how much work I had ahead of me. The nurse watched, so I smiled at her like everything was fine. She smiled back and left.

I soon made short work of the food and wanted to move on to the therapy I recognized I needed. I would set the memories, or lack of them aside, and working on building up the muscle tone and abilities I'd lost. When the body restored itself, I would begin to remember. I understood without being told, that I had to begin like a baby to exercise my limbs and I wanted to start immediately. Let's be honest. I realized I could remember something. I grasped now that I was an impatient person, at least when it came to doing things I had to be doing. I called the nurse on the call bell to ask about therapy and exercises.

"Yes?" I heard a disembodied voice somewhere over my head say. Momentarily puzzled, I then realized the voice came from an intercom.

"Sorry to bother you but when can I start therapy? I need to get my limbs moving," I explained.

"Dear, you are barely out of coma. I'm sure your doctor would want you to build up your energy first. Or wait at least until you started solid foods."

She sounded surprised and had a hint of censor in her voice. No support there. I wanted those six months back, but clearly that wasn't going to happen. Move on, I told myself. I'd wasted six months sleeping, time to fight back and get back into fighting form as they said. But who had said that?

I somehow knew I was a fighter. I'd have to do everything myself; something I knew I always did. But how did I know that?

I thought about what would work, and what limbs need to work. My hands needed to a work out. Okay, they need to grip. How do you make hands stronger?

You give them something to grip. Squeezing something soft, medium soft, would work. Where to get something to work my grasp? I couldn't even get out of bed. My limbs were useless, absolutely useless. My hand shook in weakness, from forcing the stupid thing, to do its job and feed me.

All of this began to feel hopeless. ..No, I wasn't some stupid helpless female. I had to figure out a plan. You're on your own, I told myself, nothing new. You can overcome any odds. Think, Sharron, think!

How about some finger exercises? Slowly working each finger, and then in tandem, I would get back movement. I began the exercise I devised. It sounded so simple when I had thought of how to exercise the hand, but painful and tiring. Work through the pain, I told myself. Isn't that what you've always heard?

I forced myself to do the exercises for what seemed like hours, until I couldn't take the pain any more. Then I decided to exercise my arms. Gripping well enough to pull myself up to the bar over my bed, I reached I'm with my right hand to grab the pole. My fingers won't cooperate. My fingers are weakened and my grip slipped. Damn it! Even simple exercise was impossible.

"Nothing is impossible," a voice spoke loudly in my head. But whose voice did I hear? My memory had fled, if it was ever there. I only comprehended the voice had been someone I loved, and respected. Was this a father, or a father figure? I knew I was bone weary, and a great sea of lethargy stole over me. It would be counterproductive not to take a nap, I reasoned. Surely a short nap would restore my energy and I would begin again.

I closed my eyes soon I began dreaming. At first the dream appeared happy. I viewed myself in a beautiful home and grinning at someone I couldn't see.

I smiled and felt great joy, but the sky grew dark and I found myself outside on a field. The moon overhead slowly covered by clouds, and I grew terrified. Something was wrong. The faceless man chased me once more. I ran over rocks and streams and more rocks. He kept coming and coming. I knew he'd soon be on me. He nearly had me when I willed myself to wake up saying… *This is a dream and I want to wake up now!!!*

I awoke gasping for air like I had been running a marathon. A strange man sat by my bed. His hair appeared dark, practically black, greasy, and slicked back. He had black thick glasses that he peered over like they were a prop.

An oversized suit coat in plaid and matching pants completed the picture. Despite his harmless appearance, he struck terror to my heart. What gave me the idea he put on this persona, like a piece of new clothing? I think it was his face which seemed to give it all away, like he tried too hard to portray someone he wasn't.

As I gazed at him, he jumped from the chair he sat and exclaimed…, "About damn time you woke up out of the coma Sharron. I thought you laze there forever."

He then continued, as if choosing his words carefully, "Oh Sharron, this is the most wonderful day of my life." Then he pulled me to him, fiercely.

"Let go of me, this instance. Who do you think you are? I said don't touch me! And quit acting and looking around there's no audience for your play," I blurted out, before I stop myself.

"Sharron that's not funny. Quit joking. You always had a wicked sense of humour, but I'm not laughing." the man stated, sounding annoyed and grabbing my wrist.

"I said let me go, and I meant every word. Now kindly take your hands off me," I demanded at the top of my lungs, struggling unsuccessfully to free myself of the grip, he now had on my wrist.

Taken back by my yelling, he let me go, but he still continued to treat me, like a bug under a microscope. Suddenly switching gears, his face changed. It was if a curtain went down over his face. He took on a concerned look and then a hurt look. I admit he nearly had me fooled.

I started thinking I had forgotten a boyfriend, but surely I wouldn't suffer from such bad taste.

He wasn't my type. He seemed quite violent too. I wouldn't have been so foolish to get mixed up with a weirdo like him! Would I?

"Sharron quit staring at me that way you're making me uncomfortable. I'm not amused here...Wait a minute you're not kidding .You don't recognize me at all. You don't recognize your fiancé?"

I recognized somehow that he was put on an act. No, I wasn't engaged to him. If I had been it would boggle my mind. He had to be lying, I decided. Why I didn't know, but I knew he lied.

I had no sparks with him. In fact something about him gave me the creeps. He repulsed me and made my stomach hurt. He certainly didn't sound sincere. He put on an act ... but why? He grabbed my wrists again, once again in a vice grip. I struggled valiantly, but his grip tightened and I couldn't handle his fierce clutch in my weakened stated.

"Let me go you, caveman. I don't know you and what is more, I don't ever want to know you," screamed at him fighting frantically.

"Sharron you cut me to the quick. Why do you say such things to me?" he whined, letting go of my wrist, but gripping my arms even tighter.

Maybe it was because of my dream, but suddenly I was terrified. Why did they leave me all alone with this crazy man? Where was everyone else? Couldn't they hear me shouting?

"Let me go. Let me go....Don't touch me," I yelled at the top of my lungs, and then screamed, hysterically "Help me someone help me."

As I started to pull harder frantically to be free he stilled held fast. What kind of evil demon had me in his grasp? I tried to bite him, but that was impossible; finally in the answer to my screams were footsteps running. Seconds later a nurse and Doctor Andrews entered.

"Let my patient go immediately. I said let her go," Doctor Andrews growled, pulling the man's arms behind his back.

I breathed a sigh of relief. I was safe. Doctor Andrews had saved me.

"I wasn't hurting her! What kind of a man do you think I am? Gee, I have more bruises than her. She acted crazy, so I grabbed both her arms to calm her," the man explained, sounding plausible.

Surely Doctor Andrews and the nurse who followed him in, didn't believe his act?

"Your technique doesn't seem to have calmed her, but it certainly frightened her," Doctor Andrews said, checking my blood pressure and heart rate.

"You can't tell me what to do. She's my fiancée I can speak to her anyway I want," complained the man, loudly.

"You've upset my patient. Her blood pressure and heart rate is elevated as well. This is not good for my patient, so I can tell you what to do. What is your name?" demanded Doctor Andrews.

"Titus Brown is my name and Sharron is my fiancée," the man replied a little too quickly.

Doctor Andrews consulted his clipboard. He pointed to it and then announced, "This is the approved register and you're not on the list. Leave now, Mr. Brown, or I'll have security escort you out of the facility."

"I'm not going anywhere. Who do you think you are?" Mr. Brown showed his true colours, I thought. They would trounce him faster than you could say Jack Robinson.

"Mr. Brown, so far I've been pleasant. The nurse has already called for a security guard. I suggest you leave now and don't come back, or you will find yourself with a trespassing charge and jail time," Doctor Andrews said through his teeth.

"I'll be back with my lawyer and you'll be sorry," Mr. Brown menaced.

Two security guards entered and forcefully removed Mr. Brown from my room. I began to shake like a leaf. I tried to stop, but I grew frightened. Someone had tried to kill me and that is why I was in the hospital. What if it was Him, Mr. Brown?

They wouldn't let him take me when he talked to his lawyer? Would they? Words I hadn't want to share, spilled out of my mouth, first in torments, and then at a screeching level.

"I don't know who the heck he is, but I do know I don't know him. I'm not his fiancée. Don't let him come back lawyer, or no lawyer. I don't want to see him. Someone did this to me! I wouldn't be surprised if the person was him!" I guess I appeared a little too hysterically and forcefully, because the next thing that occurred was Doctor Andrews plunged a needle into me.

"Please, please don't. It's not necessary, really. I'll be good," I pleaded too late.

"It's a little sedative. I don't like your colour, your blood pressure, or your heart rate. You've had a nasty scare and your body isn't able to cope with this right now. Calm down now," he said comforting "Go to sleep."

"I think I hate you," I replied vehemently.

"That's okay, you can hate me if you need to," he answered, smiling.

Damn him and his handsome smile! Something about the grin, made me want to smile back and tell him all my secrets.

"Don't leave me alone. He might come back," I pleaded as I drifted into a deep drugged sleep.

~0~

If you enjoyed the excerpts from A Penny Saved A Murder Earned or Dreams Can Kill please buy a copy at Amazon in Paperback or Kindle. Also please check out my other titles.

PARANORMAL TITLES:
Love's Labours Won
A Tiger's Heart Wrapped in a Player's Hide
Reborn – a novella~ prequel
MYSTERY
A Penny Saved A Murder Earned
A Diller A Dollar A Really Dead Scholar
Betty Blue Lost Her Holiday Shoe
The Kelly Murder Mysteries-Book 1-3
A Stitch in Time-prequel
Dreams Can Kill
SHORT STORY NOVELLAS
Murder Most Fowl
Jack be Nimble
ObsessionX2
The Stuff of Nightmares
Paranormal
Day of the Dead
CHRISTMAS
Christmas is Calling
A Christmas Card
The Christmas Angel
Visions of Sugarplums- all Christmas stories in one
POETRY
A Poetic Touch - The Human Condition
COMING SOON:
MYSTERY
Stray Bullet~ the story of a sheriff combatting the murders f his entire staff on his first day and a drug ring selling fentanyl

Book 4 of the Kelly Murder Mysteries – *What Will Poor Robin Do?*

Thank you for reading this story. If you have enjoyed these stories, please think about leaving me a few words of review at your favourite retailer.
Sincerely S.G.Lee

S. G. Lee